THE STATEMENT

An innocuous white Peugeot makes its way around the monasteries and abbeys of Southern France. No one would suspect its driver of being the target of commando hit-men, the gendarmerie's most wanted criminal or a public enemy sentenced twice to death *in absentia* for wartime crimes. For over forty years this fugitive has been sheltered in his own land by both Church and State. But now that he is becoming a *cause célèbre*, and the net is closing in, what other collaborators lurk in high places, dreading exposure? Brian Moore, whose writing combines profound literary intelligence with the most compelling story-telling, has unearthed the political minefield that is the legacy of post-war France.

THE STATEMENT

BRIAN MOORE

CHIVERS PRESS
BATH

First Published 1995
by
Bloomsbury
This Large Print edition published by
Chivers Press
by arrangement with
Bloomsbury Publishing plc
1996

ISBN 0 7451 3777 6

British Library Cataloguing in Publication Data available

Photoset, printed and bound in Great Britain by
REDWOOD BOOKS, Trowbridge, Wiltshire

FOR JEAN
encore et toujours

CHAPTER ONE

R did not feel at home in the South. The heat, the accents, the monotony of vineyards, the town squares turned into car-parks, the foreign tourists bumping along the narrow pavements like lost cows. Especially the tourists: they were what made it hard to follow the old man on foot. R had been in Salon de Provence for four days, watching the old man. It looked right. He was the right age. He could be the old man who had once been the young man in the photograph. Another thing that was right: he was staying in a Benedictine monastery in the hills above Salon. It was a known fact that the Church was involved. But R was not yet sure. He could not be completely sure that the old man was Brossard until he saw him claim the letter. It had been posted from Paris two days ago. For the past three days R had sat in a café across the street from the Bar Montana on the Rue Maréchal Joffre. Each afternoon the old man would arrive at the Montana a little after two. He would order a coffee and sit, reading *Le Monde* from cover to cover. The afternoon post was delivered to the Montana at around three o'clock. Brossard, if the old man *was* Brossard, had paid no attention to the post's arrival. Each day at about three-thirty he left the Montana and walked down to the Place St Michel where his little white Peugeot was parked. On the way, he stopped at a patisserie and bought a *tarte aux amandes*, which he unwrapped and ate, sitting in the front seat of his car. He would then drive out of town, going up into the hills on the lonely road that led to the Abbaye de St Cros. When

1

the monastery gates opened to receive his car, he remained there for the night.

R had been told the letter would most likely arrive at the Bar Montana on May the 2nd. So on May the 2nd, which was the fourth day of his watch, he did not sit in the café across the street, but went into the Montana, took a table in the rear and ordered a sandwich and a beer. The old man was sitting at his usual table near the door. That afternoon, the postman came in at five minutes past three, went up to the bar, called a greeting to the barman, got the barman's signature on a form, then left half a dozen letters on the bar counter. R saw the old man look back towards the bar as the postman went out. The barman sorted through the letters, took one from the pile and put it beside the service hatch. When he saw this, R got up from his table and went to the bar. He asked the barman for change, saying he wanted to play the pinball machine. He walked over to the service hatch while the barman counted the change, saw the letter's Paris postmark and the typewritten address: 'M. Pouliot, Bar Montana, 6 Rue St Michel, Salon de Provence.13100'. Pouliot was the cover name Brossard used for his post. R then went to the pinball machine down by the toilets. He began to play, nudging the machine from side to side to make the steel ball fall into the proper slot. On his third game, he saw the old man get up, walk back to the bar and say something to the barman who nodded and pointed to the letter on the service hatch. When the old man picked up the letter, R stopped playing pinball and went back to his own table. He put money on the table to pay his bill, all the time watching the old man. He saw him open the letter, look inside, then take out a *mandat* and study it. R

2

knew that the *mandat* was for 15,000 francs. Brossard—for there was now no doubt that he was Brossard—put the envelope in his jacket pocket and picked up *Le Monde*. He read for a further twenty minutes, then slipped a 2-franc piece on to his saucer, tucked the newspaper under his arm and went out into the street.

R followed him outside. As usual, the street was crowded with tourists and, as usual, R had trouble keeping the old man in sight. At the corner of the Rue Maréchal Joffre, the old man turned down a steep, narrow street and, following his usual route, went towards the car-park and his car. When he reached the Place Bourbon, he went into the Pâtisserie Du Midi and stood in a small queue waiting to buy his usual *tarte aux amandes*. R lingered under a plane tree, nearby. Today, unlike the other days he had waited here, the buying of the tart seemed to take at least ten minutes. He tried to reduce his tension by doing a deep-breathing exercise, but it didn't work. When, at last, the old man came out of the shop and went into the car-park, his wrapped cake dangling daintily from a string attached to his finger, R moved ahead of him, going into the same car-park. His rented car was one row away from the old man's Peugeot. The old man would now sit in his Peugeot and eat his *tarte aux amandes* before driving back to the monastery. Yesterday, R had decided that, when the time came, he would drive out of the car-park ahead of the old man's car and put himself in the proper place, well ahead of the Peugeot. But what if the old man did not drive back to the monastery? What if, now that he had received the money, he moved on to some other hiding place? It was a chance R could not afford to take. He would have to wait

3

until the tart was eaten, follow the old man out of town, pass the little white car somewhere on the main road out of Salon, keeping it in sight, making sure that it followed him up the lonely hilly road that led to the monastery. Two days ago, R had driven along that road, picking his spot at a place high up, where there was a sharp turn, a deep ravine on the left, and a rocky promontory on the right.

His rented car was parked on the edge of the car-park outside the shelter of plane trees. Now, when he got in, it was hot as an oven. He sat, sweating, the car doors open, watching the old pig, one aisle over, eating his tart, the crumbs, unnoticed, sticking to his chin. R unzipped his briefcase and looked inside at the sheet of paper with its typewritten message and then at the revolver. He put the briefcase on the passenger side of the front seat, leaving it unzipped. At last, he saw the cake wrappings being thrown carelessly out of the Peugeot's window and heard a grating sound as the old car's engine came to life.

R followed the Peugeot out of Salon in a line of traffic, slow as a funeral procession. Yesterday, when he followed the old man, he was careful to let other cars move in ahead of him. Today, because of his worry that the old man might not go back to the monastery, he felt it necessary to stay directly behind the Peugeot.

Four miles out of Salon, R moved ahead of the old man's car. It seemed safe. Brossard was definitely *en route* to the monastery. There was a moment of tension when R turned off, up the narrow hilly road that led to the Abbaye de St Cros. But as his car climbed up to the first bend in the road the little Peugeot, innocent as a mouse, came into the trap. R

4

then accelerated, driving recklessly, to get well ahead and prepare his move. After a further two miles, he came to the sharp bend in the road, the steep ravine on the left. At this point, the monastery was only a mile away.

R drove off on to the rough shoulder and opened the bonnet, propping it up to show that he had engine trouble. He reached into the front seat, took his opened briefcase and went out into the centre of the road where he stood, waiting.

In the empty landscape of this high desert all was deathly still. The sun beat down on the rocks like a punishment. He listened. First, he heard the faint croaking of cicadas and then, like a kettledrum's thump, the sound of distant thunder. And now, at last, he heard the slow complaint of the motor as the little white Peugeot climbed into view. R licked his lips, but his lips stayed dry. He stood, rehearsing his lines like an actor. The little car was now only thirty yards away. He held up his briefcase, waving it, and saw the Peugeot slow down, then come towards him at a crawl. He lowered his briefcase, creased his face in a smile and walked up to the car.

'Sorry,' he said. 'But, you see—' He pointed to his car. 'Are you going to the monastery? Can you give me a lift?'

The old man looked out at him. There was no air-conditioning in the little Peugeot, so all of the windows were open. The old man nodded, as if agreeing to his request. R saw that there were still some sticky crumbs on the old man's chin. He went up to the car, carrying the open briefcase, lifting it as if to tuck it under his arm. Instead, he reached in, felt the gun and took it out of the briefcase. He looked at the old man as he did this. The old man, his face

5

expressionless as a statue's, looked back at him, looked at the gun, then, without haste, deliberately pointed a heavy black revolver out of the front window of the Peugeot, holding it with both hands, firing, firing. R felt the shock of the first bullet in his chest. He fell as the second bullet struck him, again in the chest. His revolver, dropped from his fingers, skidding across the white dusty road.

The old man opened the front door of the Peugeot, got out, walked stiffly across the road and, with the ease of long experience, put his gun to the back of R's head and delivered the *coup de grâce*.

The dead man had fallen on his briefcase. As often happened, when the final bullet was fired at close range the corpse twitched and shifted position. It was then that the sheet of paper inside the briefcase came into view. It was sticking out of the flap. Monsieur Pierre did not touch it but went back to the Peugeot and took a pair of yellow rubber kitchen gloves from the glove compartment. He put them on and stood for a moment, listening. There was no sound of traffic on the road but his ears were no longer keen. Be quick. He walked back to the corpse, took the sheet of paper out of the briefcase and slipped it, unread, into his side pocket. He then picked up the revolver that had been dropped on the road and put it, with the briefcase, back in the dead man's car. Summoning all his strength, he took hold of the corpse by the ankles. There was a lot of blood. It left tracks on the road as he pulled and tugged the body towards the car. He stopped to catch his breath. He did not know if he would have the strength to lift the corpse into the front seat. It took time, but he managed. He listened again. All quiet. He leaned in beside the corpse and, careful not to get blood on his

6

clothes, took the dead man's wallet. There was also a passport, a foreign one. He put the wallet and passport into his side pocket. The car keys were in the ignition. He started the car's engine. Before he put the car in gear, he looked at the dead face but it told him nothing. He had dragged the body face down across the road and now it was a bloodied mess. He leaned in, adjusting the wheel, then put the car in gear, pulled off the dead man's shoe, jammed it against the accelerator and managed to get out of the car as it started to move forward. It went over the edge of the ravine and fell seventy feet to the rocks below. He stood, looking down at the great cloud of dust, waiting to see if the car would catch fire. It did not. Pity.

He turned and walked back to the Peugeot. Very few vehicles used this road, but still. He stripped off the yellow rubber gloves and pulled them inside out before putting them back in the glove compartment. He started up the car and drove on.

*   *   *

Yesterday, when I came out of the Montana and saw him across the street, I walked very slowly and waited. He came all the way down to the *parking*. And today when I came out of the patisserie, there he was. And there he was again, waiting for me, waving his briefcase.

He drove slowly on to a point where, at a turn, he could stop the car and look back down the winding ribbon of road. There were no cars coming up. He reached into his side pocket and took out the foreign passport and the typewritten sheet of paper.

7

STATEMENT

COMMITTEE FOR JUSTICE FOR THE JEWISH VICTIMS OF DOMBEY

This man is Pierre Brossard, former Chief of the Second Section of the Marseille region of the *milice*, condemned to death *in absentia* by French courts, in 1944 and again in 1946, and further charged with a crime against humanity in the murder of fourteen Jews at Dombey, Alpes-Maritimes, June 15, 1944. After forty-four years of delays, legal prevarications, and the complicity of the Catholic Church in hiding Brossard from justice, the dead are now avenged. This case is closed.

Monsieur Pierre looked at the passport. He opened it, and looked at the face. Then the name. David Tanenbaum. Age forty-two. He was filled with a sense of reliving his life, of going back to that former time, when he was the master of documents, when the passport or identity card, handed to him across his desk, meant that he could decide its owner's fate.

The assassin's wallet contained 6,000 francs and a Canadian driver's licence made out to David Tanenbaum. There were no credit cards, no other documents. Monsieur Pierre transferred the 6,000 francs to his own wallet then put the dead man's wallet, the passport and the typewritten sheet of paper into the glove compartment of the Peugeot, together with the bloodstained rubber gloves and his revolver. On the Peugeot's instrument panel he had affixed a Saint Christopher medal, purchased in Marseille in 1943, the day after he requisitioned Lehman's car for his personal use. It was a beautiful

8

little medal, sterling silver, showing the bearded saint fording a dangerous stream with the Christ child on his shoulders. Saint Christopher: the patron saint of travellers. In that era, many of those medals could be seen on car instrument panels as a protection against accidents. Monsieur Pierre had bought the medal and had it blessed. Somehow, it had helped to take away the feeling of sitting on a Jew's seat. Since then the medal had been transferred to the instrument panel of each car he had owned. Today was once again a proof of Saint Christopher's protection.

The road narrowed, becoming little wider than the cart track it had been for centuries. Ahead, as the little car wound around hillsides covered with row on row of vines, there came into view, shimmering in the afternoon heat, the high, ancient walls and great stone roof of the Abbaye de St Cros. As the little car approached the heavy wooden gate of the main entrance, it sounded its horn twice. Slowly, the gate was drawn open revealing a long inner courtyard, its ancient paving uneven and sown with wild flowers. The little car bumped unsteadily across this yard and entered the stables where two tractors, a little Deux-Chevaux van, and an old Panhard four-seater were parked beneath a loft filled with hay.

These were the vehicles of the monastery. No visitors. Good. He looked back and saw the gate being closed, the great iron bar lifted into its socket. The abbey was a fortress, built in the fourteenth century and, like the Benedictine abbey at Metz, one of the founding sites of Gregorian chant. He knew about such things. He had been a guest in so many abbeys, retreat houses, presbyteries, over the years, had listened to so many accounts of the triumphs and trials of religion, of saints and miracles and holy

9

deeds. He was at ease in religious houses, be it in a *curé's* parlour or the magnificence of an archbishop's palace. But it was in monasteries that he felt most at home. There, hospitality to strangers was the rule, passed down through centuries of the Faith, a reminder of a time when the Church was a power, independent of any authority, free to grant asylum to any fugitive it chose to aid. Behind the monastery walls, the world did not exist. The monks did not watch television or read newspapers. That was the most important thing. Especially now.

He locked his car. He went through the main cloister and down the shaded walk which led to the *père hospitalier*'s little office. There he found Father Jérôme, a bent little man of his own age, peering into the blue screen of a computer.

'Ah, Monsieur Pierre,' Father Jérôme said, not looking up. 'You wish to see me?'

He did not sound pleased at the interruption.

'Yes, Father. I'm moving on. Some family business.'

In the Abbaye de St Cros, he felt especially secure. The Abbot, an old friend, had long ago instructed the *père hospitalier* to make accommodation available to him at any time, day or night. Even now, after years of visits, Father Jérôme knew him only as Monsieur Pierre. He did not enquire about the nature of this family business. He was not interested.

'Safe journey, then,' Father Jérôme said. 'Will you be leaving in the morning?'

'Alas, I must leave this evening.'

Father Jérôme nodded and typed something into his computer. The interview was over.

He went out and walked past the chapel, bowing his head in reverence as he did. He went across the main courtyard, at one end of which was a large workshop where the monks made pottery which was shipped out to distributors in Dijon and Paris. He went through the empty refectory and climbed a flight of stone steps to the round turret where visitors were lodged. His room was at the top, right under the roof, low-ceilinged, with thick stone walls, a single bed, a prie-dieu, and a rough wooden armchair. There was a basin for washing and the usual crucifix on the wall, near a narrow slit of window which gave a partial view of the monastery's bell tower. He always travelled with three suitcases containing his clothes, documents and mementoes and, as there was nowhere to hang clothes in these monkish cells, he also carried a plastic wardrobe which, as a rule, he positioned just inside the door. Monastery doors did not have locks. The wardrobe made it difficult for anyone to enter without warning. On the prie-dieu he had placed a reproduction of a seventeenth-century painting of the Virgin Mary and beside it his missal, bulging with mass cards and devotional pictures.

He sat on the narrow bed and took his pulse. He felt light-headed and out of breath. This was not like other times, other dangers. It was no longer just a question of hiding from the police and the courts. His deadly enemies had come close, closer than ever before. They had known he would be in the Bar Montana, waiting for the letter. How could they have known that? Who were they, which group, a French group or the Americans? He looked again at the passport. Canadian. It could be false. I must lie down for a moment. Be calm. Be calm.

Again he saw the stranger coming towards him lifting the briefcase, taking out the revolver. If I had let my guard down after all these years, if I had lost that sense of being followed? But God be thanked, He protected me today, as He has always protected me in the past. I must give thanks tonight at Devotions. But no, I can't stay for Devotions. Some vineyard worker passing above that ravine will see the car. And the police will come here, for this road leads only to the abbey. Get up. Pack.

But when he had disassembled the plastic wardrobe and repacked his clothes, again he felt light-headed and unwell. He went down the winding steps of the turret and into the refectory. Some of the lay brothers were peeling potatoes. He asked for help and a Brother Rafael, a strong-looking fellow, came up with him and helped him with the suitcases. The third suitcase contained his collections and, as the lock was old, he thought it prudent to carry that one down himself. If it were to fall open there were the flags and other German regalia including some valuable items, all of it very saleable memorabilia. He did a small trade in such things.

It was after five o'clock when the little Peugeot was finally loaded and ready to depart. Devotions were at six and, as he knew, the Abbot would come down into the main cloister between five-thirty and six to walk and say his office. So at five-twenty he went up to the Abbot's study and knocked on the door. A voice called out, 'Yes?'

'It's Pierre, Father Abbot. Could I have a word. Just for a moment?'

'Come in. Come in.'

The Abbot's study was a large bare room, dominated by a rough wooden desk on which sat two teak trays, overflowing with correspondence. Behind the desk, in a high-backed chair like a church pew, Dom Vladimir Gorchakov, tall, bearded, austere, a

12

heavy iron crucifix stuck like a dagger in his belt. 'Well, Pierre, what is it?'

'I just came to thank you, Father Abbot. Once again I've presumed on your hospitality. However, I'm leaving this evening. I think it's time to move on.'

'This evening?' The Abbot registered surprise by a theatrical raising of his eyebrows. 'That's rather sudden, isn't it? Any special reason?'

It was best to say nothing. Invent an excuse.

'I've just been advised that a new *juge d'instruction* has been given my dossier and is complaining that the police have not been sufficiently diligent in their search. I feel that from now on it would be wise to move every week or two.'

'There have been other *juges d'instruction*,' the Abbot said. 'I'm sure you will survive this one. Although, what you tell me does clear up a point. It's something I didn't want to worry you with. But, the fact is, I've been informed that, because of this new and intense media interest in your case, the Cardinal Primate in Lyon is starting his own investigation. He's set up a commission of laymen—historians—to find out why so many of us have supported your cause over the years. So I may shortly be receiving enquiries about your visits.'

'Then it's better that I leave now?'

'Perhaps. But don't forget you're always welcome here.'

'Thank you, Father Abbot. The Cardinal Primate—Cardinal Delavigne—he's not one of us, is he?'

'Indeed.' The Abbot rose, as if to terminate the conversation. 'Safe journey, then. And God speed.'

'Thank you, Father Abbot. Thank you for everything.'

13

*　　*　　*

He wanted to be well on the road before dark. His night vision was not good and spectacles no longer seemed to help. As a young man he had been too vain to put them on, especially when in uniform. Now, he believed he was paying the price for that youthful vanity. Of course, in those days he had a role to keep up. He was a young standard bearer in the New Order the Maréchal spoke of, one of those who, in a France destroyed by its own weakness, saw the mountain to be climbed, the slopes to be conquered. And it was normal for him to feel vain: women found him handsome. Nicole had told him his eyes were 'piercing blue'. His hair was blond, his skin white and smooth. In the years he worked in liaison with Gestapo Commander Knab, Knab said his looks were 'pure Aryan', the ultimate compliment in Knab's view. And, always, he had seemed younger than his years. 'A good-looking altar boy', was how that Belgian bitch described him to the Paris Sûreté. That was in '53, when he was thirty-four years old.

He remembered, though, that spectacles came in useful in the Paris years. He and Jacquot wore tinted glasses each time they went out on a job. Jacquot said they were a sort of mask, he said people remembered only the tinted glasses when they tried to describe you afterwards. And it was true. He still kept a pair of tinted glasses in his car and now, as the monastery gates were pulled wide and the evening sun shone straight into his windscreen, he drove out, then reached into the glove compartment to find them. They were lying under the bloodstained rubber gloves. The gloves must be washed: the passport and the sheet of paper he would show to the

14

Commissaire. The Commissaire was an expert on these groups.

It was fifty odd kilometres to Avignon, an easy drive. The road leading down from the monastery was empty of traffic. When he came to the turn in the road and the ravine, he drove very slowly but did not stop. There could be police or an ambulance down there. Because he did not stop, he was unable to see if the wreck had been discovered.

When he reached the main road he turned in the direction of Avignon. At the first garage he pulled in and asked if there was a pay telephone. He was in luck. While they filled the Peugeot's tank he went into the phone booth and dialled the Avignon number.

A woman's voice. Madame Vionnet? 'Who shall I say is calling?'

'Just say Monsieur Pierre. Thank you, Madame.'

He was not expected. It had been laid down long ago that he would make contact only in a case of emergency.

After a long delay he heard footsteps on an uncarpeted floor.

'Hello, yes?'

'It's Monsieur Pierre, sir. I'm in the area. I was wondering if I could drop in this evening and show you a Belgian Congo issue, 1875, Congo Free State. The portrait is of King Leopold II. They're beautiful stamps, sir. Would you be interested?'

The Commissaire seemed irritated. 'Where are you?'

'I've just left Salon, sir.'

There was a pause. Then: 'I'm just about to have dinner. Well, all right. I could see you for a few minutes at, say, nine o'clock.'

'Thank you, sir.'

Nine o'clock meant driving in the dark. Shit! I must find a room somewhere close to his place, some tourist motel. I can use my Pouliot identity card if they ask to see one. They won't. They don't check on you nowadays, the way they used to. Still, staying in a hotel is never wise.

He arrived in Avignon shortly after seven. It was still light. He drove first to the Avenue Delambre, passing the Commissaire's modest pink stucco villa, one street away from a big Leclerc supermarket in an anonymous suburb, just outside the medieval walls of the city. He had last been there, when? Eight years ago? In the street next to the supermarket he saw what he wanted, a motel on the edge of a roundabout. He went in and reserved a room. They did not ask him to fill up a form. He left a suitcase in the room then drove back up the Avenue Delambre. In the Leclerc supermarket there was a snack bar. He ordered *saucisses*, *frites* and a beer. He would have preferred the *steak-pommes frites*, the special of the day, but his dental bridge was loose again. It was endless the trouble his teeth had given him, not only in pain and discomfort, but also because he had to be careful about dental records. If you have no official identity you get no health benefits. It was only in the past few years, through the good offices of Dom Adelbert at Montélimar, that he had been at last getting proper dental treatment.

In the snack bar when he picked up his plate of food, he chose, as usual, to sit with his back to the passersby. Halfway through the meal, he felt sick and felt that he was going to throw up. It had been too much for one day. Not only the Jew and the excitement but then the other bad news. If I'd not gone in to see the Abbot this afternoon, would he

16

have told me about this new ecclesiastical inquiry? Maybe not. Because now, no doubt about it, I'm an embarrassment, even to those who know true right from wrong. With this inquiry starting, more doors will close. Cardinal Delavigne is part of the post-war Church, Gaullist, resistant, reformist. And no one can stop him, he's the Primat des Gaules.

The Commissaire would expect him to be on time. He left the meal half eaten, got into the car and drove along Avenue Delambre. He parked one street away from Number 129. It was already dark. He waited until his watch said nine, exactly nine, then got out, locked the car and walked up the little pathway that led to the front door. A dog began to bark. He was afraid of dogs. He looked around, hoping the dog was shut up inside.

When he rang the doorbell, someone called out to the dog. The barking stopped. The door was opened by Madame Vionnet. He saw that she did not remember him. Nor would he have known her, this white-haired old woman in running shoes and a purple track suit, she who had once sat behind a desk in the Commissaire's private office, twisting her long legs into a lock, showing the tops of her stockings, smiling like a whore.

'I have an appointment,' he said. 'Monsieur Pierre.'

There was no sign of the dog. It must be in the back of the house. When he entered the hall, he had to squeeze past some twenty cardboard cartons of wine, stacked almost to the ceiling. He saw the trademark on the boxes: Caves des Saussaies. Côtes du Ventoux. What did a top Parisian *flic* do in his years of retirement? The Commissaire had bought a small vineyard near Vaison la Romaine. The joke was in the trademark. Rue des Saussaies. Where they beat the shit out of me.

The whitehaired woman showed him into a small front parlour, also encumbered by cartons of wine. The dog barked again and he heard the Commissaire's voice. 'Balzar!' The barking stopped. The Commissaire came into the parlour, picking his teeth with a wooden toothpick. He had aged in these past seven years. In his green cardigan and blue corduroys, his skin weathered by the sun and burned to a dark reddish colour, his fingernails black as a peasant's, he could well be the humble winegrower of this latest deception. Only his eyes remained unchanged. They did not blink.

'You were in Salon? Did you receive your envelope?'

'Yes, thank you.'

'Something wrong, then?'

By his tone of voice, the Commissaire made it clear that this visit was not welcome.

'Yes,' he said. He had rehearsed his story in the car as he drove up tonight and now he told it succinctly. When he had finished, he took out the assassin's passport and the sheet of paper. The Commissaire, who had been standing until then, gestured to him to sit, and sat himself, switching on a table lamp to examine the passport.

'It seems genuine,' he said. 'But I'll keep it and make a proper check. You're a lucky man. You might have been at the bottom of that ravine this evening.'

'Not lucky, sir. I first spotted him yesterday afternoon when I came out of a patisserie.'

The Commissaire put the passport into the hip pocket of his overalls. 'So, what do you make of this,

18

Monsieur Pierre?'

He knew that when the Commmissaire addressed him as Monsieur, he intended no politeness. The title was a code name. The Commissaire's tone was contemptuous.

'That's what worries me, sir. Whoever this group is, they knew I would be in Salon. They knew I would be in the Montana. They may even have known that I was waiting to pick up that envelope. What do *you* make of it, sir?'

'I don't know this group,' the Commissaire said. 'They're not the usual. They may be a Jewish student group, or relatives of the Dombey people. I'll look into it.'

'But how would they know about the envelope? No one knows that, not even my friends in the Church.'

The Commissaire discarded his toothpick, placing it delicately in an ashtray. 'By the way, you were staying at St Cros, were you?'

'Yes.'

'And you told them you were leaving this evening. Did you tell them what happened?'

'No.'

'Good. This is something that shouldn't be talked of outside this room.'

'Yes, sir.'

'So, what are your plans now? Where will you stay?'

'I think, Aix, sir.'

'You *think*?'

'I'm sorry. It was just a manner of speaking. I'm going to spend a couple of weeks in the Prieuré St Christophe, outside Aix.'

'You are expected?'

'No, but I'm always welcome there. The Prior is a friend of the Chevaliers.'

'Write down the address. And the telephone number, if you have it.'

The Commissaire took a ruled exercise book from a drawer in a side table. 'The Chevaliers,' he said. 'Good. From now on, as you know, you'll have to be doubly careful. You're losing friends.'

'I know.'

'And after Aix?'

'I'll move on to Villefranche, sir. And then to Nice. There, I have no doubt of my welcome.'

'Friends of the ex-Archbishop of Dakar?'

'Yes, sir.'

At that moment, Madame Vionnet put her head around the door. 'Did you want coffee, Henri?'

'In a moment,' the Commissaire said. 'My guest is leaving now.'

He stood up. Monsieur Pierre stood also. The Commissaire led him out into the crowded hallway. Monsieur Pierre pointed to the wine cartons.

'How was the *vendanges*, sir?'

'Good. Bit crowded in here at the moment. I'm shipping these cases out tomorrow.'

'Caves des Saussaies,' Monsieur Pierre said and smiled. 'I remember.'

The Commissaire opened the front door and turned his unblinking eyes on his visitor. 'Of course you do. You did a lot of singing there.'

Monsieur Pierre did not answer.

'Good-night,' the Commissaire said.

'Good-night, sir.'

*   *   *

20

As the Commissaire closed him out into the darkness he looked back and saw Madame Vionnet at the window of the front parlour, pulling down the blind. He waved to her. She gave him a small polite wave in return. Her name is Rosa. Does she remember me? Was that why she asked about the coffee?

He had kissed her once. In that selfsame Rue des Saussaies. It was on the day she told him that he could go and that no one would interfere. The Commissaire and his two assistants were out to lunch. A police orderly had brought him from his cell, delivering him to the Commissaire's office for a further interrogation. The orderly then, surprisingly, left him alone in the office with the Commissaire's sexy secretary, she who later became Madame Vionnet. She had taken dictation at some of the previous interrogations. He had heard the *flics* call her Rosa. Rosa it was who told him the Commissaire was out to lunch, then settled back at her desk, locking her long legs in a sexy pose, smiling at him, rearranging a small bowl of flowers on her desk. He had been arrested six weeks earlier. Denis, who had been arrested some days before him, had given him to the police. They had come for him, finding him in a maid's room in the Rue Monge, folding and unfolding counterfeit banknotes to make them seem used.

'Condemned to death *in absentia*, former Chief of the Second Section in Marseille, you know what's going to happen,' Commissaire Vionnet had said. 'You'll be transferred back to Marseille and, about three months from now, you'll be taken out and shot. Well, what else can you expect? That's the way things are today.'

What choice did he have? First they beat the shit

21

out of you. Then the announcement about Marseille. And then the question, 'Tell me. What do you know about the clergy's political activities at present?' He had to tell them something and it had to add up. He had named names, some of those who had hidden him, some who belonged to the MAC. But Commissaire Vionnet wanted more.

'Abbé Feren, you knew him?'

'Of course. He was the almoner of the *milice*.'

'But after the Liberation, when he went into hiding you met him, didn't you? He hid you?'

He had to say yes. It sounded as if they had arrested the Abbé. They had been looking for him ever since his condemnation *in absentia*.

The Commissaire was blunt. 'It will be a great help for your case if you can tell us where we might find him.'

Of course it was a sin to tell, it was a sin he would never forgive himself for committing. He wasn't sure where the Abbé was, but he made a guess. It pleased the Commissaire. It was an accurate guess. The Abbé was arrested a week later in Sanary. He was sentenced to seven years. Of course, seven years was only seven years. He was supposed to be living in Italy now.

Yes, there was no doubt about it: the police found him a co-operative witness. Commissaire Vionnet was pleased, more than pleased. Other questions came up. Discreetly. Only when he and the Commissaire were alone. A question about deportation orders signed by someone very high up in the *préfecture* in Paris. Orders he had helped to carry out. He had told the truth. What had he to lose?

The Commissaire said nothing. He offered no hope. But his manner changed. And then, two days before he was due to be transferred to Marseille, he was brought up from his cell and taken to the Commissaire's office at an hour when everyone was out to lunch. Left alone with the Commissaire's secretary, who called him a *beau mec* and locked her legs in that sexy way. Smiling, showing her bare thighs. She winked at him. She opened a drawer and took out a belt and a pair of shoelaces, things they took away from you when they brought you in. 'Fix yourself, so you won't look like a prisoner.' He got the point. When he had laced up his shoes she told him, 'Wave to the guards. You're going to lunch. Now, give me a kiss goodbye.'

She wanted to be kissed, so he had kissed her. He walked out of the office, along the corridor, down the staircase and out into the yard, passing the guard house, taking care to wave to the guards, as she had told him. He was wearing a clean shirt, a belt around his trousers and there were laces in his shoes. He looked like an employee. And then, a moment later, he was walking down the Avenue Marigny, a free man. And what did he do? He went straight into the nearest church and, on his knees, thanked God for his deliverance. God had helped him once again. God who loved him, who understood him, who protected him from his enemies.

It was dark outside. The street lamps were not working properly. Nothing worked properly any more. What could you expect? A country full of foreigners, ignorant *beurs* shacked up in slum bidonvilles on the edges of every city, filthy *noirs* fed and cared for by our government while honest French people can't find work.

He drove back to the motel. It was only when he had undressed and knelt to say his prayers that he remembered. Now that his enemies had found him in the Bar Montana, he could not pick up his envelope in Salon when his next payment came due. He should have asked the Commissaire about that. Still, the next payment was two months away. Plenty of time to find out. He made the sign of the cross, closed his eyes and again thanked God for His protection. God had not wanted him to die today. God had warned him, had given the gun into his hands. It was self-defence, but still he had, once again, taken life. A Jew could not go to heaven. He remembered a discussion with Monsignor Le Moyne, his confessor. The Monsignor advised him that it was a Christian action to give money for a mass for the dead Jews of Dombey. He did not understand the Monsignor's point of view. But still ... a mass had been said on his behalf. Monsignor Le Moyne was a saint, of course. But practical. It was he who decided: 'Yours is a special case. The State has taken away your right to live a normal life. It has forced you to become a fugitive. It has judged you without hearing a word in your defence. As I see it, you have been obliged to do some of the things that you have done.'

That was after his confession, a confession in which he had told the Monsignor, his confessor, about the Paris years, about the car hold-ups he and Jacquot had carried out, one a failure, one a success. And about the traffic in counterfeit francs, the black-market coffee racket, and what else? There were so many things one had to do to survive: there were so many of us hiding out in those years just after the 'Liberation'. The betrayal, we called it. The old Maréchal in exile in Germany, camping out in Sigmaringen castle while de Gaulle marched down the Champs-Elysées pretending that he, and not the

24

Americans, had freed France, what sort of freedom was it, it was a time of communists, a time of revenge, the 'Purification', they called it, the communists were out for blood: trials, accusations, people thrown into prison, women's heads shaved, execution squads. Darnand, our chief, God rest his soul, he didn't run away to Germany, he didn't pretend: he stood before those red-robed judges in the Palais de Justice. 'Monsieur le Président, I'm not one of those who's going to tell you I've played a double game. I did what I did. I am proud of what I did. I made a mistake but I acted in good faith. I believe I served my country.' Yes, Joseph Darnand was the only one to speak out for the things we fought for, a hero, a man of courage. In his prison cell in Chatillon the night before he died, he wrote a letter to de Gaulle, asking clemency for 'my *miliciens*, for these old soldiers of 1914-18, and these many young men, workers, peasants, and boys from the liberal professions who did not hesitate to give up everything to serve what they considered from the bottom of their hearts to be the true interests of their country. They have committed only the fault of loyalty to a great soldier, they have been almost the only ones who refused to betray their oath and abandon a lost cause.'

Next morning they took Darnand out and shot him. I am old now, I forget things, I have to make lists, I write down names of new people when I meet them, while the names of old friends go blank in my mind. But I will never forget those words. The cause was lost—more than that, the war was lost. Was it any worse to live under the Maréchal's New Order in co-operation with the Germans than to watch the Anglo-Saxons, the stupid '*Amerloques*' and the two-faced English who ran away in 1940, help Russian

25

communist troops rape and steal and kill their way across Europe? How many in France knew then that we had not won but had lost the battle? How many sensed it but didn't dare to say it? The Church knew: in Rome, Pius XII asked for an amnesty for all who had been faithful to the Maréchal. The Pope knew the real enemy. He knew that the Maréchal was first and always a true son of the Faith. Soon even the stupid Americans saw the light and began to use Nazi brains in the struggle against Stalin. We could speak our minds at last. The enemy was Russia. The true motherland of those who brought France down.

I am on my knees tonight, humbly giving thanks for God's mercy today. I must not let my mind drift back to anger. I have been a sinner and now I am blessed with God's pardon, God's love. He does not want me to die. I will protect myself against my enemies, His enemies.

He made the sign of the cross and stood up. He opened the suitcase that contained his memorabilia and took out the Walther pistol from its leather holster. Whoever sent that Jew to kill me knew that I would be in that bar in Salon today. Why was I there? To pick up my envelope. Who are they that they would know about the envelope, the most secret thing, the thing I have confided to no one, not even to Monsignor Le Moyne? What else do they know? Who told them?

It was a long time since he had slept with a gun under his pillow. He had lived in the shadows, for forty-four years, managing to stay in France when others fled to Argentina or Peru. That had been his triumph. He had not let them drive him out of his own country. He had lived here under their noses. But now they would find him. Someone knew. And,

26

in that moment, fear came upon him like an ague. If I die tonight, will I be forgiven? Will God balance the things I did to save France from the Jew communists against my sins: women, the friends I betrayed, the hold-ups, the frauds? Monsignor Le Moyne says God's mercy is infinite. I have lived these years of old age as devoutly as any man: mass, prayers, devotions. Yes, I killed today, but in self-defence.

But the fear did not leave him. What if the Monsignor is wrong? What if God, weighing all in the balance, casts me down? I must make my confession to Monsignor. He will absolve me. I must change my plan. Tomorrow, I will drive to Caunes.

CHAPTER TWO

Security, they called it. T had never seen anything like it. He looked out now across the Place de l'Alma, at the tour Eiffel, wrapped in grey fog, at people waiting for the 63 bus across the street. Why here? Why this particular café, a tourist place full of foreigners eating salads and drinking beer? Maybe that was why. There were no regular patrons in a place like this. It was his second visit. Yesterday, when they made the first rendezvous with him, he had been told that his contact would carry an English newspaper, *The Times*.

A 63 bus came down Avenue Président Wilson and stopped opposite. And suddenly he sat up straight, for there was the contact getting off the bus, the same man, carrying the newspaper. Security, they called it. Someone had been reading too many *romans policiers*. Why can't I know this guy's name, why can't I meet him without all this fucking around? We're on the same side, aren't we?

The contact, carrying the newspaper, came into the café, walked along among the booths and tables and stopped as if by chance. 'May I?'

T nodded. 'Of course.'

The contact was a man in his fifties; he could be a doctor or a lawyer, respectable, bourgeois, with a snob accent which T found irritating.

'You got them all right?'

T took the little plastic envelope out of his anorak. The contact slipped the three photographs out of the plastic and looked at them carefully. 'You made sure of the size?'

'Of course,' T said.

'How old are you?'

'What's that got to do with it?' T hated these questions about his age. OK, so he looked like a kid. He was not.

The contact sighed. 'For the passport,' he said.

'Sorry. Twenty-five.'

'Good,' the contact said. He slipped the photographs into his pocket. A waiter came and the contact ordered an *express*.

'And for you, Monsieur?' the waiter asked.

'Same thing,' T said.

As the waiter walked off, the contact looked around. T could see that he wasn't used to this. He probably *was* a doctor or a lawyer. Somebody's uncle.

'I've been told to give you an address,' the contact said. 'Memorize it and, after tonight, forget it. We're taking a risk, a security risk, by putting you in touch with this person but he wants to meet you. What he tells you may be a help. The address is 6 Rue St

Thomas d'Aquin in the seventh arrondissement. It's behind a church. The Métro is Rue de Bac—'

'I'll find it!' T said.

'It's apartment 5, on the fourth floor. If you arrive at seven, exactly seven, and ring the bell, you can go straight up. Oh, by the way. I hear you'll be leaving at once. Maybe tonight?'

'One thing,' T said. 'I don't want to ask questions, that's understood. But those photos. Does that mean I'll be leaving France?'

'You'll get your instructions tonight. The passport will be ready. We'll work on it this afternoon. Got that address?'

'Of course.'

'Good. I'll leave you now. Pay for my coffee, will you? Good luck.'

What had luck got to do with it? You had to know what you were doing. As Pochon said, you'd better grow eyes in the back of your head. Pochon wasn't like this contact today, he'd never say, 'Good luck.' What Pochon said was, 'Look. I'm the one who's working with this organization, not you. The less you know about them, the better. They aren't in the milieu. They're politicals. I've told them you can do this job, that's all they need to know. I'm your contact. If you're arrested I'm the only one you can get into trouble.'

Pochon was in his sixties, an ex-*flic*. Retired with the rank of inspector. He'd break your legs if you got *him* in trouble. 'I'm behind you,' he said. 'All the way. But remember. Do as I say. Obedience saves lives.'

When T left the Place de l'Alma, he went to Janine's apartment in the Rue St Joseph. Janine worked in Le Printemps, in the glove department. He thought that was stupid. She didn't need to work in a

29

boring job. Her parents were in couture, they owned a firm that made fancy buttons for big names like Lacroix and Saint Laurent. They were well able to support her. But she didn't get on with her mother. So she said. T didn't want to know all that shit. It was her business, not his. Today, as he let himself into her apartment, he thought it would be nice if you could deal with girlfriends the way Pochon dealt with him. No confidences, no family histories, no questions asked. Not that he told Janine what he was doing. He was a medical school dropout, he told her. He told her he was living off his parents. He said he wasn't proud, like her. He took an allowance from them and spent it. 'I bet you do,' Janine said. 'They must be rich.'

*   *   *

For the last few weeks he had been staying at Janine's place. Now, when he went back there from the Place de l'Alma, he wrote her a note, saying he'd ring her sometime after nine. He went on from there to the little room he rented in the Hôtel Terminus where he packed a bag with what he'd need. Then, to kill the time before his meeting, he went to see a film that was playing on the Champs-Elysées. It was an American film, guns, guns, guns, a load of rubbish. But he liked American films. Lots of bullets. Cars crashing into each other. Actors bouncing around like acrobats. Nothing to do with real life.

*   *   *

It was beginning to get dark when he arrived at 6 Rue St Thomas d'Aquin. It was the real old style, a

30

building with a big dark courtyard. He walked across the courtyard and looked up. There were very few lights on in the apartments above. There was no name on Apartment Number 5. He rang and at once the buzzer sounded, letting him in. There was no lift, but there was a good carpet runner on the wide flight of stairs. The names on the apartments on the second and third floors were French. No foreigners. No offices. When he reached the fourth floor there were two apartments, both with handsome mahogany front doors. One of the doors was open and an old man stood there, waiting. He was wearing a brown cardigan over dark evening trousers, a formal evening shirt, black tie. His hair was grey and he had a grey moustache. He didn't look Jewish, but then, T thought, a lot of Jews don't look Jewish, especially if they're *bon chic, bon genre* like this one.

The old man didn't introduce himself. He simply said, 'Come in.'

The apartment was large. T saw, ahead, a drawing room with two wall niches containing Roman busts, crossed swords on a wall, antique lamps, good heavy old furniture, Turkish carpets and rugs, oil paintings of classical scenes and, on a table in the front hall, a jumble of silver-framed photographs. The largest photograph was of a chic wedding. The bride and bridesmaids wore short frocks, thirties-style. Beside the wedding photo was one of an officer in a dress uniform. It was a photograph of his host.

'This way,' the old man said. He led T through the drawing room. In a dining room off to the side, T saw a large mahogany table set for six, with an elaborate floral centrepiece, crystal glasses for four different kinds of wine, heavy silver service plates. With this sort of set-up there must be servants. But there were

31

no servants in sight.

'In here.'

The old man now opened the door of a room with leather armchairs and sofa, walls lined with books, a library ladder stretching to the ceiling, a great teak desk littered with papers. Old money, T decided. If he's Jewish, he's Jewish like the Rothschilds.

'Please sit down.'

The old man now went to the big desk and took out a large manila envelope. He brought it to T, taking from it a passport, a set of plane tickets and a French driving licence. The passport was dark blue with *CANADA* in gold lettering on the front. He opened it at a page showing T's photograph and a name: *Michael Leavy*.

'Sign on the opposite page of the passport. Signature of bearer. Michael Leavy. That's also the name on the driver's licence and your airline ticket. You know about this, of course?'

'Yes.'

The old man leaned back in his chair. His brown cardigan fell open revealing a black cummerbund over the top of his evening trousers.

'You're very young. I was expecting someone older.'

'I'm twenty-five.'

The old man had a soft charming voice and smiled each time he spoke. 'We're sending you to Aix,' he said. 'There's a flight leaving Paris at nine o'clock tonight. When you arrive, go to the Eurocar rental desk and a car will be waiting for you in the name of Michael Leavy. Brossard is staying at this address.' He handed T a sheet of ruled paper with a handwritten address. 'He should arrive there tomorrow. He drives a Peugeot.'

'Yes, I know. A '77. White.'

'He will stay in the residence adjoining the boys' school, which is the address I've just given you. In a week or two he may move on to Villefranche or Nice. I don't know what you've been told. I mean, I don't know your *modus operandi*.'

'I've been briefed,' T said. 'It's up to me, when and where.'

'I see. Well, let me just say one thing to you. This individual is old but he is a fox who knows perfectly well how to go to ground. If he gets your scent, he will disappear and, believe me, you won't find his tracks. We mustn't let that happen.'

'Right.'

Why did I have to come here? Why did he want to see me? Is that all?

And then, as if he had spoken aloud, the old man said, 'I suppose you're wondering why I asked to see you. It's against our rules. But I feel I should be honest with you. Our friends haven't told you that you're the second man to try this mission. Am I right?'

'What do you mean?'

'A week ago we sent someone from this same commando to kill Brossard. We knew exactly where he would be at a certain date. Our information was correct. He was there. In Salon de Provence, as a matter of fact. The person we sent was someone like yourself, young, trained, knew what he was doing. We don't know what happened. But we know he's dead. He was shot and his car was tossed into a ravine. We'd given him a false passport like yours. It wasn't on his body. The statement—you know about the statement?'

He now took from the manila envelope a large

33

typewritten sheet of paper and held it up. T nodded.

'It disappeared. It wasn't found with the body. We've had a discussion about this. Apparently, your friend the Inspector hadn't informed you about it. That's why you're here tonight. I know it's up to you when and how you do it. But I felt you should be told—everything. You must kill him on your first attempt. You may not get a second chance.'

He stood up. 'Thank you for coming. And don't forget.' He held up the typewritten sheet. 'This *must* be found on his body. People must know why we did it.'

He paused. T heard voices in the outer hall.

'Those are my dinner guests.' The old man took off his brown cardigan and picked up a dinner jacket which was lying on the leather sofa. 'If you'll come this way, I'll let you out by the rear entrance. There's a service stair. Sorry about this. People usually arrive late. These guests are early.'

The back stairs were dark and narrow. The flight was at nine o'clock. He would have to take a taxi to the Hotel Terminus to pick up his bag, then go straight out to Orly.

On the Boulevard St Germain it was raining. He started to run, looking for the nearest taxi rank. He was lucky. There were two taxis waiting. It was only when he was sitting in the taxi, crossing over to the Right Bank, that he began to think about what he had been told. And about the Inspector. Why didn't the Inspector want him to be warned? Why ask? *Flics* always lie. What Pochon said was, 'This man is seventy years old, he's been hiding out for forty odd years. He's not expecting you. He never was one of the hard ones in the *milice*, he was a paper shuffler, the head of the second section. He made up lists of

34

people to be arrested and shot but he sent others out to do the shooting.'

No warning. Not a hint that he'd already sent someone down to do the job. Sent him to Salon where this old paper-shuffler shot him dead. How much are they paying Monsieur l'Inspecteur, these Jews? How much is he charging them for me?

It was eight-thirty when he arrived at Orly. He went to a phone booth. Janine answered.

'Where are you? I thought we were going to meet at the Pergola?'

'I'm at the Gare Montparnasse,' he said. He hadn't even thought what he was going to tell her: a lie came more quickly than the truth. It was normal: everyone lied in the milieu. 'It's my father,' he told her. 'He's had a heart attack. He's in hospital in Bayeux. Maman rang me this afternoon.'

'I knew it,' she said. 'I've had this bad feeling all day. I've just read your horoscope. I'm sorry about your papa. When will you be back?'

'I don't know.'

'Shit! Next Tuesday is your *fête*. I'm not supposed to tell you but we were planning a surprise party. What do you think? Should I cancel it?'

'What's this about a horoscope?' he said. Horoscopes were no joke.

'It's just a horoscope in *Elle*. It's silly. I shouldn't have mentioned it.'

'What did it say?'

'I don't remember exactly.'

'*What did it say?*'

'Oh, it was something like, "You have to make a sudden trip and lose out on pleasures." I thought that meant the party. It sounds like it, doesn't it?'

'Wait a minute,' he said. 'Get it and read it to me.

35

Hurry. I've got to go.'

He waited. There was something bad in the horoscope. He knew it.

'Here we are,' she said. 'Virgo. With a seventh house, Saturn, in your solar return chart being echoed by a full moon in Pisces, this is a dangerous time for you. You will have to make a sudden trip and lose out on previously planned pleasures. Beware of strangers on your journey. As Mars moves to Leo on the 9th you will be forced into an action that could do you great harm. If possible you should not agree to a proposal that others have made to you. This is no time to play the hero.'

'Is that it?'

'Yes. It's funny, isn't it, about the sudden trip. I hope everything goes all right with your papa. And listen. Phone me on Sunday. I won't cancel the party until I hear from you. Take care.'

'I will.'

On the plane he took out the sheet of ruled paper and looked at what was written on it: *Prieuré St Christophe. Avenue Henri Martin 6, Aix-En-Provence. Telephone: 42 96 17 36.*

Underneath this address someone had written in a tiny tight handwriting:

Cistercian residence, adjoins Cistercian boys' school. Prior, Dom André Vergnes. Sixty-five. [In touch with Chevaliers.] B should arrive there August 10. He is expected to stay *circa* fourteen days, then plans move to Villefranche, then Nice. Drives white Peugeot, 1977. In Aix, the Café La Mascotte, Place des Tanneurs, is where he goes most afternoons. Uses this café's address as a poste restante.

36

He took his bag from under the plane seat and opened it to the folder. There were two photographs. The first, a black-and-white head-and-shoulders of the subject, showed a young man in a dark suit, white shirt, dark tie, pointed ears close to his head like an angry dog, frizzy blond hair, light-coloured eyes. Underneath, pasted on the border of the print, a hand-lettered notation: *BROSSARD. 1946.* He stared at the face. French. Pure blood. Not like me. He looked at the second photograph. The slip of paper with it said it was seven years old. There were two men, an old priest and another old fart, white-haired, in a cardigan. He studied the old fart's face. The same close-set ears, the same stupid stare. Now he's supposed to be seventy, he should be dead, he's part of history. The *milice*. Those days are old movies, that's all, Nazi uniforms, propeller bombers, *Casablanca* with Ingrid Bergman, and *chez nous*, Rommel in the desert with his tanks, and the Americans landing at Algiers. Papa was a little kid in the Arab quarter in Oran, he saw Rommel's tanks on the run, then the winners, Americans, French, British, parading through the streets, he loved that, he loved uniforms, Papa, he wanted to be a soldier, a French soldier, not the ones in France, not Vichy, not the ones this guy fought for, but de Gaulle's. Not that it mattered. No matter which French side you fight for, the French will fuck you, like they did Papa, who couldn't wait to grow up and join the French army, yes, in '55, signing on in Algiers, he was twenty years old, and they filled him full of lies, he was to be a Harkis, part of an elite commando, auxiliary troops, riding camels, encamped beside the French, Papa was in the top commando, the Georges, Muslims under French officers, fighting for Salan and the

37

junta against the FLN, our own brothers. I wonder if that rich Jew officer tonight knew I'm the son of a Harkis. No, he wouldn't know that. I'm not dark, like Papa. I can always pass for French.

He looked again at the photographs on his lap. The old man could have changed a bit in seven years. But his ears will be the same. When I see him, I may only have a minute to make up my mind. So I have to be sure.

He looked again at the photograph of the young man, the *milicien*. Look at the ears, the nose, the mouth. Remember them. Remember them.

But the photograph face stared out at him, as if defying him to remember, the young man's eyes calculating and guarded as though the camera were in a police station. He looked at that face. When you think of it, this guy is like Papa. They both picked the wrong side and paid for it. Papa, who fought his guts out for the French, had to leave his own country because his people saw him as a traitor. If he'd stayed, people like him, the FLN buried them in sand and put honey on their faces for the ants to eat. Or cut their ears, lips and balls off, dressed them as women and lit them with a match and a jerrycan of petrol. And the French did nothing. They sailed home. Like the Nazis. The Nazis dumped this guy who fought for them against his own people. Papa was lucky, he didn't stay behind, he thought he was French, he thought he could live here, so he took the lousy French offer to leave with the army and sail to a country he never knew. In school they told him Algeria was part of France, stupid cunt, he wasn't French he was Harkis, native troops, an embarrassment, the French government stuck them into camps and farmed them out as casual labour and

38

promised proper jobs, proper housing, all that shit. But did nothing.

And here I am tonight, going south, to Aix, not so far from where I was born in the Harkis camp at Sète, where Papa was paid slave wages to pick grapes. Is it any wonder he did what he did? Is it any wonder I do what I do?

But that's it. People who back the wrong side lose the war. And go on losing. Like Papa, picking up the gun again, after eight years' hard labour in Harkis camps. And two years after that, shot dead in the street by French *flics*. And look at this guy, this French Nazi, condemned to death *in absentia* twice over, a traitor, forty years on the run. Even now, when he's an old man, it's not finished for him, I'm on this plane, I'm going to kill him. And he, he's waiting for me. He killed whoever came before me.

My horoscope. What date is today? The 6th. 'On the 9th you will be forced into an action that could do you great harm. This is no time to play the hero.'

CHAPTER THREE

How old was she? It was the first question Colonel Roux asked himself when he received the summons to meet her. As an examining magistrate she must be a woman of a certain age. But there was always this curiosity if one was to work with a woman. Madame Annemarie Livi. An Italian name. He had not been able to ask anyone about her. Until this news became official, it was something he was not able to discuss, even with his fellow officers. General de Bernonville himself had called Roux into his office and warned him that politics were involved. Politics at the highest level. The Commissariat of Police did not yet know that they were being dismissed from the investigation. There were sure to be repercussions. Political repercussions.

Last evening he and Claire had dined together in a little restaurant just off Rue du Four. Claire's sister, Anne-Laure, had agreed to babysit. He had waited until then to tell Claire his news. And, of course, the first thing Claire seized on was that he was going to work with a woman.

'How old is she?'

'I don't know. That's what I've been wondering. She must be getting on, if she's a *juge d'instruction*.'

'Livi,' Claire said. 'Wasn't that Yves Montand's real name?'

'You're right,' he said. 'Maybe she's his sister.'

'I hope so,' Claire said. 'In that case she'll be too old for you.'

Now, in the sunshine of a May morning, waiting in a corridor outside one of those anonymous offices near the Galeries d'Instruction in the Palais de Justice, he saw, sitting at her desk, a tall woman, elegantly dressed in a dark-green *tailleur* and a white silk blouse. In her late forties, he supposed. Her dark hair spilled over her shoulders as she bent to untie the tapes of the mass of documents that the clerk spread out on her desk. The clerk turned and signalled Roux to enter. Judge Livi stood up, smiling, her hand extended in greeting. The clerk closed the door, leaving them alone.

He liked her at once. She was direct.

'Colonel, as you know, I am the third examining magistrate to be given this case. When I read through these dossiers, I became aware of the difficulties my

40

predecessors faced. The case is baffling. We simply must take a new direction and at once. Tell me. Have you been told why I am requesting that the gendarmerie take over this investigation?'

It was a direct question. He gave General de Bernonville's answer. 'I've been told that it concerns the relations between the Commissariat of Police and the Vichy regime. It's a matter of record that the French police were pro-Pétain and collaborated with the German occupiers in deporting Jews to German concentration camps. Moreover they often acted on their own initiative before the Germans requested such aid. The gendarmerie, on the other hand, were sympathetic to the Resistance and to the de Gaulle forces fighting outside France. As a result the gendarmerie has a clean record in the matter of collaboration with the Germans. The Commissariat of Police does not. General de Bernonville, my superior, says that because of that you have decided to transfer this investigation from the police to the army.'

'Perfect summation, Colonel. You should have been a lawyer.' Judge Livi leaned back, shook her head and laughed.

Definitely an attractive woman, he decided.

She then lifted in both hands a heavy sheaf of documents as though weighing them. 'This is only a part of it,' she said. 'It would take a month to read it all. I've tried. What I find is forty years of legal obfuscation, court reports, trial delays, unsuccessful police investigations and repeated attempts by the Catholic clergy to obtain a pardon for this man. Why? Brossard is a former member of the *milice*, twice sentenced to death *in absentia* as a wartime collaborator, thief and murderer. Why?'

41

'A pardon was obtained, wasn't it?' he said. 'In 1971. Partly through the efforts of a certain monsignor.'

'You said "partly", Colonel. And that's the right word. No monsignor, or even bishop, could engineer such a pardon without some help from the Elysée Palace. That's the angle that interests me. How could they persuade the President of the Republic to sign a pardon for a thug like Brossard? And they almost got away with it. In fact, if this new charge hadn't been laid against him we wouldn't be able to touch him now.'

'You're right, Madame. That changed things. Of course, he'd have been freed in any case, when the statute of limitations for wartime crimes ran out five years ago. The question is, why didn't he come out of hiding then?'

'I suspect he was afraid of reprisals, perhaps from the sons and daughters of his victims. The same people who've launched this new charge against him, the charge of a crime against humanity for the murder of the fourteen Dombey Jews in 1944. Thank God, there's no statute of limitations on that.'

'Except for his age,' Roux said. 'He's seventy years old.'

'I know. If he drops dead before we find him, the big fish will never be brought to trial.'

'Big fish? Do you mean people in the Church?'

'No, I don't mean the Church, although the Church is involved, of course. Tell me, Colonel, are you a Catholic?'

Roux shrugged. 'Statistically, yes. Practically, no.'

'Like so many of us,' Judge Livi said. 'Neither believing nor practising. And yet we know that, within the Church—what's the phrase?—within my

42

Father's house there are many mansions. I think that's particularly true today. Everyone knows that the main body of the French hierarchy was pro-Vichy during the Second World War. There may be things that the Church still wishes to conceal. But we also know that this wasn't the whole truth. There were prelates and priests who actively supported the Resistance, hid Jews and protested against the deportations.'

'True. But I believe, Madame, the media's charge that, over the years, monsignors, bishops, even cardinals, have been involved in efforts to secure a pardon for Brossard is nothing less than the truth. The Church is heavily compromised. And they know it. That's why Cardinal Delavigne has appointed laymen to head his investigation. By the way, I've been told we may have a lead there.'

'You don't waste any time, do you?' Judge Livi said. 'What sort of lead?'

'A member of the Cardinal's commission.'

'That could be helpful.'

'Yes, but it could make things difficult for us. If the Church carries out a real investigation, priests who helped Brossard in the past may turn against him. And that will drive him deeper into hiding.'

'On the other hand, Colonel, some of them may be willing to co-operate with us?'

'I hope so. But you mentioned, earlier . . . you said something about big fish?'

'Don't you know the people I'm referring to?'

Roux hesitated. Don't make a gaffe. Let her tell me. He shook his head.

'Three other Frenchmen were accused, like Brossard, of crimes against humanity. None have been brought to trial. One of these men, Vichy's top

43

representative in dealings with the Nazi occupiers and the man responsible for the first big round-up of French Jews in 1942, here in Paris at the Vélodrome d'Hiver, managed like the others to have his case delayed time after time, and is still living in Paris, in comfort, a free man. As is the second man, the former Vichy Chief of Police. It's interesting to know that this same Vichy police chief stood for election to parliament after the war and was, moreover, a close friend of the President of the Republic.'

'I remember thinking much the same thing,' Roux said.

'As for the last of the three, he is possibly the greatest criminal of all. He's living, at liberty, in Paris, in his comfortable home, surrounded by friends and relations. He's not, like Brossard, a convicted criminal, with a long record in police dossiers. He is a Commander of the Legion of Honour, a greatly skilled technocrat, accustomed to operate at the highest level of government. He's a former Secretary General of the Department of the Gironde, a friend to several French presidents in the post-war years and was a minister in Giscard d'Estaing's government in the sixties. In the Vichy years he was also responsible, time and time again, for the dispatch to Germany of Jewish death trains.'

'Hard to believe, isn't it?' Roux said.

'Not really. All three of these men had excellent lawyers. They didn't hide themselves like Brossard. They didn't need to. They came forward, maintaining a discreet silence as the charges of a crime against humanity were read out to them. They were then allowed to go free, pending a time when their cases would be tried. I believe that, unless we find Brossard and bring him to trial, none of these big

44

fish will ever have to appear before the courts. But if Brossard *is* sentenced, public opinion can be mobilized to demand that they also be tried. And he must be tried! If he is, I suspect we'll find out that over the years presidents, prime ministers, cardinals, judges and prefects of police have all been part of this conspiracy. And unless the whole truth is brought out into the open it will for ever be a stain on the conscience of our country.'

Judge Livi leaned back and sighed. 'I'm sorry, Colonel. I know that sounds like a courtroom speech, but it's what I believe.'

Roux looked at her and smiled. 'I'm glad you do, Madame. I believe it too.'

'So, we're together on this?'

'Of course. I've already started my investigation. This afternoon I leave for Caunes, in the Languedoc.'

'Caunes?'

'Monsignor Maurice Le Moyne is living there, in retirement. He was Brossard's great champion. It was partly, if not largely, through his efforts that the famous pardon was procured.'

'Le Moyne,' Judge Livi said. 'But why should he help you? Or do you have something else in mind?'

'The charge of the crime against humanity has been laid by a Jewish group, under the direction of Serge Klarsfeld, the lawyer who found Klaus Barbie and brought him to trial. They are actively searching for Brossard. The Simon Wiesenthal Centre, which is, as you know, the most successful and wide-ranging Nazi-hunting group, is also intensifying its efforts to find him. These are law-abiding groups who will act in a law-abiding manner. But there seems to be another group involved. The DST, which monitors terrorist activities, has intercepted two

45

telephone conversations which reveal that what seems to be a Jewish commando is plotting to assassinate Brossard, because they believe he will never be brought to trial. If that's true, we've got to act quickly.'

'Interesting,' Judge Livi said. 'Why wasn't I told about this?'

'The DST is a branch of the National Police. They don't want to see the gendarmerie succeed where they've failed.'

'So they didn't inform you, either?'

'No. But we have our sources. And if there *is* a Jewish commando trying to kill Brossard, I can use that information to convince his clerical friends that we are the least dangerous of his pursuers. Brossard himself may not be swayed by such an argument. But Monsignor Le Moyne? I think it's worth a try.'

'And when do you leave for Caunes?'

'I have a flight to Montpellier at three o'clock.'

'Then, perhaps we can have lunch together before you go?'

'That would be a pleasure, Madame.'

CHAPTER FOUR

Nowadays, Monsignor Le Moyne was obliged to wait for lifts. He had been offered one by Jean Marie Bouchard, a winegrower who had business in Carcassonne. It was a chance to see Roger Dufour, an old schoolfriend, a lawyer *en retraite* and living there. Four days in Carcassonne: it had been a pleasant change from the medieval silence of Caunes. Not that he had any desire to live again in cities. He had, he sometimes thought, two sides to his nature, each perched like an angel on his shoulders. On the left was the dark angel, ambitious, fond of the trappings of the Lyon archbishopric, the pleasant meals, the good wine, the Renault 25 at the door, the attention one received when announced as Private Secretary to the Cardinal. He had served under three cardinals, not, of course, in a truly important position. He was not a principal secretary, but a more humble functionary, one who arranged episcopal meetings and schedules, a screen for interviews, sometimes almost a valet who dealt with details of the Cardinal's wardrobe and arranged for his medical check-ups. As Private Secretary, in Lyon and later in Rome, he had been able to use the prestige of the Cardinal's name to further his long crusade to obtain a presidential pardon for Pierre Brossard. The crusade was, he suspected, congenial to his dark angel: not, of course, that it was ignoble work. But there was in it, perhaps, a hint of personal ambition, some hidden desire to be seen as the saviour of others and a healer in the cause of national reconciliation. He had always had a weakness for that role of saviour. Monsignor Maturin, Vicar General of the Diocese of Lyon, once said of him that he had set himself up as 'a welcoming committee for every form of distress'. That was true in the days before he took up the cause of Pierre Brossard. It was also true that as Cardinal Villemorin said of him, he later seemed to have made Brossard's cause 'his principal aim in life'. Indeed, he had spent the past two decades in an endless round of correspondence with leading religious and political figures, visits to those who might help by testimonials, studies of legal documents, appeals for Christian charity and forgiveness for his protégé. He had occupied himself with these matters to a point where in forgetting the life of the spirit he had incurred the disapproval of the angel on his right shoulder, the white guardian angel of his soul.

* * *

The white angel, of course, approved of his living in Caunes. The retreat house here was like a small monastery. The Sisters of l'Enfant Jésus, who ran it as a home for retired clerics, belonged to an old-fashioned Order: the nuns wore long habits, confined themselves to work and prayers within the convent walls and obeyed the local bishop in every way. Caunes, a village which had changed little in appearance over the centuries, was a daily reminder of that true France, *La France profonde*, of values, beliefs and customs fast disappearing in this end-of-century turmoil. In Caunes, in the silence of the village church, he would kneel for hours, ignoring the pains of his joints, his eyes fixed on the altar, seeking, through prayer and meditation, to forget his efforts to save Pierre and instead to enter a state of devotion in which he, Maurice Le Moyne, had no wishes, no ambitions, save to worship Jesus Christ, Our Lord.

These last days of his life, in the broken corridors of memory, Rome and Lyon came rarely to mind. What had he accomplished in his life as a priest? In truth, nothing seemed to have succeeded. Nothing. Perhaps, over the years, he had managed to show a few sinners the light of God's grace. There were those who had profited from his counsel, yes. But to take credit for bringing sinners back to God was in itself a sin: the sin of pride. And to be honest, that had not been the driving force of his ministry. His dream of national reconciliation, of obtaining a pardon for his protégé which would serve as an example of how we French must forgive and forget the errors of our country's past, had, in the long run, failed, failed completely. And yet he had been skilful, resourceful and tenacious. Not for nothing was he the son of a former President of the Marseille bar. He had himself studied law before entering the priesthood and those legal skills had served him well in his crusade. How much of his life had he wasted, yes, wasted, on that crusade? Imagine: to have achieved success on the highest level, a pardon signed by the President of the Republic himself, and now to see it, years later, in essence revoked. The enemies of national forgiveness had once again triumphed. Poor Pierre was now hounded more than at any time in the past. The Jews want my hide, Pierre always said. And alas, he's right. Not that I can say that today. We must forgive our enemies, especially the Jews. Now, I am ashamed of the things I said against them long ago. Impossible to criticize, after seeing what I know to be the truth: the films of the mass graves, the naked, emaciated bodies, the Nazi soldiers with their guns. The numbers of dead are exaggerated, no doubt, but what matter? Sin is sin in any number.

*   *   *

Bouchard, the winegrower, had picked him up on the outskirts of Carcassonne shortly after 2 p.m. Bouchard, a widower with two teenaged sons, one of whom had been in trouble with the police over possession of drugs, was grateful for help Monsignor Le Moyne had given as a character witness when the

49

boy's case came up before the magistrates. Now, as he had many times before, Bouchard returned obsessively to the subject of the immigrant population. He blamed the Muslim element in his son's school for the boy's involvement with drugs. 'Le Pen is right,' he said. 'Send them back where they came from. What do you think, Father? Wouldn't you vote for Le Pen, if you were me?'

Monsignor Le Moyne stared at the road ahead.

It was after five when they arrived in Caunes. Bouchard kindly dropped him at the door of the retreat house. It had begun to rain and as he rang the bell, he huddled under the porch, trying to keep dry. He felt very tired. He would go straight to bed after supper.

'Monsignor, welcome. How was your journey?'

'Pleasant, Sister. Very pleasant.'

'We're glad you're back. Your friend Monsieur Pierre has been waiting for you for two days now. We didn't have your address in Carcassonne. Poor man, he's very anxious to see you. He's staying at the Pension Medicis. And, oh! Someone else telephoned earlier today. A Colonel Roux. We told him we were expecting you this evening. He asked us to let him know as soon as you returned.'

'A colonel?'

'Yes, Father.'

'And how are you supposed to get in touch with him? Did he leave a telephone number?'

'Yes, Father. Just a moment. I'll get it for you.'

He watched her go into the little office off the hall. What colonel? And what was Pierre Brossard doing in Caunes?

'Here you are, Father.'

He looked at the slip of paper. A local number.

'May I use the phone, Sister?'

Alone in the little office, he dialled.

'Gendarmerie.'

At once, he put down the phone. A week ago Dom Adelbert had telephoned him from Montélimar with two disturbing pieces of information. 'Maurice, have you heard from the archbishopric recently?'

'No. Why?'

'I've been told that Cardinal Delavigne is sending two of his staff on a warning trip, with photographs of our friend. They are visiting convents, presbyteries, monasteries, anywhere they believe he was given lodging in the past. They show his photograph and ask that he be turned away.'

'That's disgraceful.'

'Well, things have changed. Delavigne has to fend off awkward enquiries. The media are on the hunt, as you probably know.'

'But still,' he had said. 'We haven't lost all support, have we?'

'I hope not. But the direction of the inquiry has changed. I hear, on good authority, that a new *juge d'instruction*, a woman, by the way, has transferred the investigation from the police to the gendarmerie. The gendarmerie were always hostile to the Maréchal.'

'Exactly so.'

'So you may be receiving a visit from either source, the archbishopric or the army. I thought I'd better warn you.'

And now this; only a week since I received that call and here he is, some colonel lusting for promotion, already at my doorstep. And Pierre is here, in the same village at the same time. *And* staying at a *pension*. That's odd. Why didn't he stay with Abbé

51

Fessard at Peyriac, just up the road? Did Fessard turn him away?

He felt his hand tremble as he searched the telephone book for the number of the Pension Medicis.

'This is Monsignor Le Moyne speaking. Do you have a Monsieur Pouliot there?'

'Yes, Monsignor. I'll get him at once.'

He waited. The gendarmerie could be keeping a watch on this house to see if I have returned.

'Monsignor? Pierre here. I'm so happy you're back. I know it's late, but may I come round? Perhaps we could have supper together? There's something I have to tell you.'

'Pierre, listen to me. I'll meet you down at the church. Kneel at the back, near Our Lady's Altar. I'll sit in the bench behind yours. Don't look at me, please. We may be watched.'

The thing about Pierre, as Monsignor Le Moyne well knew, was that he never, ever, lost his sense of caution. 'Yes, Monsignor,' he said. 'I'll go there straightaway.'

Caunes was not much visited by tourists, even now in the height of the summer season. As Monsignor Le Moyne walked through the narrow streets he saw only Madame Malet closing up, taking in the baskets of vegetables and fruit from the stall outside her shop, and old Pellerat, a pensioner, sitting on his usual bench near the fountain. He was reasonably sure that he was not being followed. As he approached the church his footsteps sounded ominously loud on the cobblestones. Now that, suddenly, he felt the breath of the gendarmerie on his neck, he could at last imagine the life Pierre led all these years, always looking and listening to see if he is being followed. Just imagine those former times when, he tells me, he only ventured out at night. Imagine a life lived on false papers, a life in which one must constantly move from place to place, a life spent alone, dependent on the support of convents and monasteries, never knowing whether the next priest or Mother Superior you ask for asylum will welcome you in a spirit of Christian charity or turn you away in disgust.

And now he's in greater danger than ever before. To have gone, from a case unknown to the public in the years before the pardon, to today's *cause célèbre*, forever in the papers. I remember he wrote to me recently, saying that he has counted up the number of times his name has been mentioned in *Le Monde*. Over four thousand times, he says. And it will never end. Never, until he dies. God has pardoned him his sins. Of that I am sure. But his enemies will not.

As he approached the church he saw Durand, the sexton, hosing down the path behind the graveyard.

'Good evening, Father. Warm, isn't it?'

'Yes, indeed. Is Father Cadras taking confessions this evening?'

'Yes, Father.'

That would mean the church would not close early.

'Thank you, Durand.'

There were five people in the church. Two women kneeling at the side altar where candles were lit for good intentions. At Father Cadras's confessional, a solitary man knelt, waiting his turn. Pierre sat, partly hidden by a pillar, facing Our Lady's Altar in the side aisle.

Monsignor Le Moyne went up, genuflected and sat in the bench behind him. He said, in a whisper, 'Pierre?'

53

'Father. We are being watched?'

'I'm not sure. I'll tell you about it later. Why have you come here? I thought we decided we shouldn't see each other for a while.'

'I had to come. It's strange that I should be kneeling here in a church because I have to make my confession. It's urgent. And I must make it to you.'

'That's not so. Any priest can hear your confession. It's foolish for you to have come.'

'I've just killed a man. You're the only one I can tell.'

'Who did you kill?'

'A Jew. A Jew who was sent to kill me. It was self-defence, but still ...'

He has killed a Jew. And a colonel of the gendarmerie is here in Caunes, asking to see *me*.

'What happened?'

The familiar voice began to whisper. When it had finished, he asked, 'But what were you doing in Salon? How did these people know you were there?'

'I have no idea, Father. I was staying at the Abbaye de St Cros, outside the town. I often stay there. It's a very safe place. The day before this happened, I sensed I was being followed. But I wasn't sure. As you know, it's easy to become nervous about such things. Especially now.'

So he carries a gun. He was prepared to defend himself, even to kill. That's not in keeping with his promise never to take life again. Is it possible that he lies to me, as he is forced to lie to others? If what he says is true and the Jew was about to shoot him, he committed no crime in defending himself. But sending the car and the body over the ravine?

'Pierre, we have talked about this many times. I know how you feel about giving yourself up. I've

54

always respected your wishes, but now—listen to me—the passport and this paper you mention, you kept them, of course? Don't you realize that, if you give yourself up and show these documents to the police, most people will see that you are being persecuted? That the Jews want to kill you and that they are behaving like common murderers. It may be the perfect moment for you to come forward, at last.'

As he said this, he watched Pierre sitting in the seat ahead of him, silent, staring at a statue of the madonna which was lit by a halo of electric light bulbs. Pierre was an old man now, his hair white, his neck and face scored with deep lines, his clothes shabby, a darned green wool cardigan, worn corduroys, heavy workboots. In his hands, as always when in church, he holds a rosary. I know he is devout, I know he is truly repentant, I know he has lived a blameless life for the past forty years. How could I have helped him if I had not believed in his repentance? And yet, yesterday, he killed someone. And now asks God's forgiveness.

'Well, Pierre? Answer me.'

'Father, if I do as you say, they will try me and condemn me. I will spend the rest of my life, like Klaus Barbie, in a cell.'

'Have the police found this man's body?'

'I don't know. I'm not worried about that. I didn't come for help. I came to confess to you and to ask for absolution. They will try to kill me again. If I die now, I want to die in the state of grace. You tell me that my sufferings over the years have earned me God's pardon. That's all that matters to me. I didn't want to kill again. I was forced to do it. Did I sin in taking that Jew's life?'

'I can't answer that, Pierre. In any case, God will

forgive you. I will give you absolution.'

He said the words of absolution.

'God bless you, Father. And don't worry. I'll leave tonight.'

'Pierre, I have other bad news. There is a colonel of gendarmerie here in Caunes. He arrived this morning and wants to see me. You know, don't you, that the gendarmerie have taken over your case?'

At that moment, he heard the noise of a confessional door being closed on the other side of the main aisle. Father Cadras, the local *curé*, came out of the box, his tour of confessionals completed. He looked directly across the aisle, waved, and came over.

Father Cadras did not know Pierre, but might recognize him from the newspaper photographs. Quickly, Monsignor Le Moyne rose from his seat and crossed the aisle to shake hands with the *curé*.

'You were in Carcassonne, Monsignor?'

'Yes, indeed. Very pleasant.'

'Were you there for the demonstration against Maastricht?'

'Yes, but I missed it.'

As he spoke to the *curé* he saw Pierre rise, genuflect to the main altar and walk quickly down the side aisle, going to the side door. The *curé* paid him no attention.

'There is a lot of feeling here,' the *curé* said. 'You can't blame the local farmers.'

'People are afraid of these changes. Understandable.'

'These European treaties,' the *curé* said. 'Do you know what I think? They're schemes to put the Germans back in the saddle.'

'You could be right,' Monsignor Le Moyne said.

He heard the side door slap shut. When, if ever, would he see Pierre again?

CHAPTER FIVE

The roulette wheel had stopped and the steel ball of his luck had dropped into a losing slot. Everything was going against him. When he arrived here he went, as usual, to Abbé Fessard at Peyriac, four kilometres up the road. But the Abbé made some excuse about having a guest in his spare room. Was he, like others, distancing himself? And then to find out that Monsignor Le Moyne was in Carcassonne and wouldn't be back for two days. And now, a colonel of the gendarmerie. Here. Wanting to meet with the Monsignor. Here. In this little place where, if I turn the corner of this street, I could walk right into him. If they saw me with Monsignor in the church, they could be following me now.

But the streets of Caunes were empty. People were eating supper. There were no cars parked in the little square that led to the Pension Medicis. He nodded to an old man who sat on a stone bench outside the town hall. As he did, he saw one of the local gendarmes come out of the town hall and exchange a greeting with a man in blue overalls who was performing the usual evening routine of taking down the tricolour.

The gendarme was now walking up the narrow street a few paces behind him. He forced himself to walk slowly. The gendarme caught up with him and passed him, turning off into a street on the right. Now, the Pension Medicis was only two streets away. His Peugeot was parked in the yard at the rear of the *pension*. It would take only a few minutes to pick up his bag, pay the bill and be on his way. There was no reason for this colonel to suspect that he was anywhere near Caunes. No reason whatsoever.

As always, when he felt the dagger of fear, he worried about his heart. As always, when that happened, he tried to think of something else. He thought now of absolution. *Ego te absolvo*: those words, the most joyous in religion. He remembered, long ago, when he was a boy in Sanary, coming out after confession, and feeling a sense of triumph. Confession was the greatest sacrament of the Church, a passport out of the flames of hell. Sometimes he thought that he might not be so religious a Catholic, so devout in his duties, if he did not have the relief of knowing that his sins would be forgiven. That was why he had come to Caunes. It was worth the risk, colonel or no colonel. *Ego te absolvo*.

But these thoughts did not still his fear. He could feel his heart flutter, trapped in his chest. As he went up the lane that led to the little *pension*, he felt his pulse. Irregular. I took my pill this morning. Or did I?

When he went into the little front hall of the *pension*, the proprietress, sitting at her desk in front of a poster advertising a Montpellier music festival, looked up with a hotelier's false smile.

'Monsieur will be with us for dinner?'

'Alas, no, Madame. Could I trouble you to make up my bill?'

'You found the Monsignor, did you?'

'Yes, thank you.'

His room was on the first floor. It looked out on the yard where his car was parked. As he put his things into a suitcase, he saw, parked beside his Peugeot, a

58

black Renault with an official licence plate. The engine of the Renault came suddenly to life and it drove out of the yard. As it passed below his window, the driver turned his head and looked up.

He pulled back, stumbling over the bed in his hurry to stay out of sight. An officer in the dress uniform of the gendarmerie. He listened. The car noise diminished. There are no officers of that rank here in Caunes. Just think. He could have walked into the hall downstairs when I was talking to Madame.

He shut his suitcase, checked that he had taken his razor from the bathroom, then went down the winding flight of stairs. She laid the bill on the counter. He paid it.

'I've just seen a car go out, Madame. Was that a special licence plate, I wonder?'

'I couldn't say, Monsieur. I didn't see the car.'

'It was an officer. Gendarmerie, I think.'

'Ah, yes—let me see.' She bent over the registration book. 'Yes, from Paris. You're right.'

'It's a hobby of mine,' he told her. 'Registration plates. Anyway, thank you, Madame.'

He folded the bill and put it in his pocket.

'*Bon voyage, Monsieur.*'

CHAPTER SIX

Roux had studied the dossiers. They were remarkably complete for a subject who had no criminal record whatsoever. There had been years of reports by the police and intelligence services and even a confidential memo extracted from a source within the Elysée Palace. But the most intriguing

59

dossier on Monsignor Maurice Le Moyne had been compiled by a young historian, a member of Cardinal Delavigne's commission investigating Church involvement in the affair. Even now, with that dossier in his hand, Roux had no idea of how Judge Livi had obtained it. Yet here it was, a series of interviews, comments, a curriculum vitae: in all a psychological profile of a cleric of insignificant powers, thought by his ecclesiastical superiors to be politically naive, dismissed by the cardinal he worked for as a 'silly ass', yet who had somehow managed to manipulate and influence persons who held positions of the highest power. There was the Good Samaritan, the writer of endless letters admonishing his correspondents to remember the words of Christ: 'Forgive and you will be forgiven.' There was the relentless importuner, searching out testimonials for his shady protégé, even visiting former victims of the *milice*, to seek their aid, brazenly declaring that 'as a Christian, and a priest I dare to ask a pardon for this man'. There was the letter to General de Gaulle in which he wrote: 'It is in the name of Christ's charity and for no other motive, neither interest, nor ambition, nor constraint, nor political aim, that I have acted in this case.' But of course, as the dossiers showed, this was not the truth. In the same letter to de Gaulle, he had implied that Brossard was innocent of the crimes which he, Monsignor Le Moyne, surely knew he had committed. And in other letters to those in positions of power, he was guilty of similar deceptions. While in Rome in the sixties, serving as little more than a lowly functionary in charge of a French cardinal's housekeeping staff at the Holy See, he had sent out letters to heads of government signing himself as 'Private Secretary to His Eminence', implying, falsely, that the letter was written with the Cardinal's approval, and thus raising suspicions in the highest levels of the French government that Rome itself had a vested interest in protecting Brossard.

And now with those documents in a folder on the seat beside him, Roux was driving up a narrow street in Caunes *en route* to the retreat house in Rue Danton. He had telephoned again, at 6 p.m., and had been told that the Monsignor would, as usual, be taking supper there. Supper was at seven. He planned to arrive at seven-thirty and surprise his subject at table. There was an element of theatre involved. He wore his dress uniform, gloves and kepi. His posture would be military; never that of a policeman.

*   *   *

'Monsignor will be with you in a moment.'

The visitors' parlour in the retreat house was small and dark, dominated by a lifesized plaster statue of the Virgin Mary placed strategically opposite the solitary window so that the evening light fell like a halo on the madonna's head. He placed his gloves and kepi on the polished table and stood, facing the door. The man who entered was old enough to be Roux's father, small and frail in a black soutane and elastic-sided boots, his features settled in that mask of age that neuters its owner's sex.

'Good evening, sir,' the Monsignor said. 'I'm afraid I was away when you called this morning.'

Roux introduced himself as the head of a new investigation into the Brossard case. He was asked to take a seat.

'And so, naturally, you came to see me. They all

61

do. And, always, I have to give the same answer. I'm no longer in touch with Pierre Brossard. I believe that in joining the *milice*, he, like many young men of his generation, made a serious mistake. But I also believe that he acted in good faith. Therefore, even if I could help you, I would refuse to do so.'

'But surely, Monsignor, there's more to it than that? I know you believe that he's not guilty of the killing of the Dombey Jews. But to talk about his acting in good faith is surely naive. And, besides, there are other criminal charges against him. What about the property he stole from various Jewish families? That's on record. It's proven.'

'Colonel, the requisitioning of Jewish property was a routine action under the Vichy regime. Pierre Brossard was merely carrying out orders.'

'It's also on record that he sold jewellery, furniture and other property belonging to those Jews and put the money in his own pocket. That's the work of a thief.'

'Colonel, let me say I am not convinced that your information is accurate. In any case, Brossard was granted a pardon in 1971 by the then President of the Republic. If it were not for this new charge, a charge which is definitely not proven, he would be a free man today. This new charge is, again, an example of the way in which he has been persecuted over the past forty years. You are too young, if you'll pardon my saying so, to remember that in the period of the Occupation the Resistance was led by communists whose aim was to deliver our country into the hands of Stalin. It wasn't surprising that most Frenchmen remained faithful to the regime of Maréchal Pétain. I won't try to excuse the fact that the *milice* turned out to be an odious organization with close links to the

German occupiers. But I do contest and have always contested the accusations made against Pierre Brossard that he ordered the death of the Jews at Dombey and was responsible for acts of torture and execution against other Jews and resistants. I also know, and this you must take on trust, that he is a devout and practising Christian who has led a blameless life ever since. In addition, I believe, with President Mitterrand and most other men of our generation, that we must move forward, and put these old animosities and cries for vengeance behind us.'

Monsignor Le Moyne paused and spread his hands in an apologetic gesture. 'Sorry. I have a bad habit of sermonizing. Forgive me. But I do want you to understand my position.'

'Of course. And, knowing that, I didn't come here expecting you to tell me where I can find him. But there *is* a new development in his case, one that I would like you to consider. We've discovered, very recently, that a Jewish group has formed a commando with the object of assassinating him. Its existence has been uncovered by the Direction de la Surveillance de Territoire, a special branch of the National Police. From telephone calls that the DST intercepted, it appears that this group has inside knowledge of where Brossard may be found. His life is now in danger in a way it never was before. If he gives himself up to the gendarmerie, he will, at least, be protected from these assassins. And if, as you say, he is innocent of this new charge, he may be able to clear his name. That's why I've come to see you. Perhaps you have some method of getting in touch with him?'

There was a silence in the room. Monsignor Le

63

Moyne sat, his head bowed as if in meditation. At last he looked up, not at Roux, but at the statue of the madonna that faced him. 'And who is behind this group? Do you know?'

'No. But we know they believe Brossard will never be brought to trial. That's why they've decided to kill him.'

'You say they know where he is. How can they know that? You say they have "inside knowledge". What does that mean?'

He has taken my point, Roux decided. He's fishing. Tell him the truth. 'I don't know, Father. I'm telling you what was told to us by the DST.'

'I see.' Monsignor Le Moyne stood up and went to the window. He stood silent, then turned and said, 'Colonel, as I told you, I don't know where he is. But, I think you're right. Now, if ever, is the time for him to give himself up. In the past I've argued with him. I've begged him to come forward and defend himself. But he has developed a feeling of persecution in these years of clandestineness. He is convinced that he will not receive a fair trial. It would be difficult to persuade him otherwise.'

'Monsignor, if anyone could persuade him, you could.'

'I doubt it. And, as I said, I don't know where to find him.'

'I'm sorry to hear that. I'd hoped you might have some means of reaching him. He *is* in great danger. I'm convinced that someone who is in his confidence is betraying him to this group.'

'But why would anyone do that?'

'For money, perhaps.'

'From the Jews? That's possible. Yes.'

Roux also stood, picking up his gloves and kepi

64

from the table. 'In any event, thank you for seeing me, sir. I'm sorry to have interrupted your supper.'

'Not at all. Tell me. Supposing that, by some chance, Pierre Brossard gets in touch with me, could I have your card? And perhaps a telephone number—somewhere where you can be reached at any time?'

'Of course.' Roux unbuttoned the breast pocket of his uniform. 'Here you are. That telephone number is my direct line.'

'Thank you. By the way, are you planning to go straight back to Paris?'

'I'm driving to Montpellier tonight. I hope to fly back to Paris in the morning.'

'Well, then, I mustn't keep you.'

They shook hands at the front door. As he put the car in gear, Roux looked back and saw the Monsignor raise his right arm to wave goodbye. I think it worked. He's an old-line anti-Semite, willing to believe the worst. He jumped on that bit about the DST. That worried him.

* * *

Monsignor Le Moyne watched until the car was out of sight. Then to the telephone.

'Monsignor Le Moyne, Madame. Is Monsieur Pouliot there?'

'No, Father. Monsieur Pouliot has left.'

'When?'

'Oh, about half an hour ago.'

'Thank you, Madame.'

In the dining room across the hall he could see the others finishing dessert. His plate sat, untasted. He felt shaky, tense, his mouth dry. He walked across the hall and sat on a bench in the corridor near the toilets.

That colonel said, *I'm convinced that someone who is in his confidence is betraying him.* Who can be betraying him to these Jewish murderers? Where has he gone? Where will he sleep tonight?

After a few minutes Monsignor Le Moyne got up and went into the little front office. Sister Gonzaga was closing up a filing cabinet. 'I'm sorry to disturb you, Sister, but I must make a telephone call.'

'That's fine, Monsignor. I'm just leaving.'

When she had gone he shut the office door and locked it. He could not have someone walk in on this conversation. He dialled the number. It was a direct line. Please God, he's there.

'Yes?'

That angry, authoritative voice.

'It's Maurice.'

'Go on.'

'I have to get in touch with our friend. A Jewish group is trying to kill him.'

'Yes?'

There was a silence at the end of the line.

Then, 'How do you know about this?'

'I've just had a meeting with a colonel of the gendarmerie who's now in charge of the case. He told me the Jews seem to know where they can find him. This colonel thinks someone in our friend's confidence may be betraying him.'

'Why would they do that?'

'The Jews have money.'

'So, what do you want?'

'You have connections, sir. The report about this came in from the DST. I thought you might be able to find out who the informant is?'

'Let me give you some advice, Monsignor. Your efforts on your friend's behalf have been admirable.

66

But, in my view, he has stepped over the line. He will now be wanted for murder, not a murder of forty years ago, but one committed last week. If he's arrested, he could be tried for the murder. And I doubt, given the present state of public opinion, that his plea of self-defence would be accepted. He's on the run now, he's probably frightened as never before. I think this is the moment for you to stay out of it. Pray for him. That's all you can do. And one last thing, my friend. Remember, you made me a promise never to mention my name in connection with these events?'

'Of course. That's understood. And I'm very grateful for the help you gave us in the past.'

'I told you never to mention that help. Not even to me.'

'I'm sorry, sir.'

'Remember, Monsignor. You're a man of your word. I expect you to keep it.'

'I will, sir.'

'Good-night, then.'

'Good-night.'

CHAPTER SEVEN

Shit! A big truck pulled alongside the little Peugeot, almost banging into it as the truck rushed ahead, moving into the lane in front. Night driving, he couldn't do it any more, he had hoped to get as far as Montpellier, but now he saw a sign: *Béziers*. It would have to be Béziers. The truck's red tail lights disappeared round a bend in the road. He slowed his speed to 90 kilometres. Don't panic. Don't panic!

Is it possible to tell everything you did to a priest in the confessional and yet be telling lies? If God Himself were to ask me now what I felt back then, what I felt at the cemetery wall in Dombey, what I felt when we threw the bomb into the synagogue on Rue Daumier, would I lie to God Himself? Would I say I felt I was doing my duty? And what *did* I feel? What did I feel when I went down to Room 410 and saw Le Grange pushing their heads under the water in the bath? We needed information. He said this was the way to get it. What did I feel when I received the train orders and stood in the station supervising the loading? Those faces staring out at me from the open freight-car doors. I looked away. They were going to die. I was afraid of them. They saw me, they knew. Some day, in some afterlife, they would point me out. That's him. Brossard. He did it. He killed us.

The sign ahead said: *BÉZIERS. 10 Kilometres.*

Ego te absolvo. Am I really absolved, am I really cleansed, am I free to enter heaven? I don't know. My whole life has been an imposture. I'm lying, even when I think I'm telling the truth. Yet, in these last years, I *want* to tell the truth to someone. If I can tell it to a priest in confession, I feel better, I feel hope, if not in this world, then in the next. Confession is my insurance. My heart is bad. I could drop dead tomorrow. I *need* absolution. If God forgives me then I don't give a damn about this world. I'm finished with this world. The proof is, I put my neck in danger by driving all the way to Caunes to hear those words from a priest. I could have gone directly to Aix and been safe in my bed tonight instead of out on this road, my bones aching, driving half blind, afraid as I never was in the days when I was just small fry, one of hundreds of *collabos* sentenced to death *in absentia*.

68

Now, I'm a *cause célèbre*, my name in the papers, people have seen that photo of me when I was twenty-six, someone might have an epiphany in the street and shout out, 'Eureka, it's Brossard!' And now they've got this new judge, Livi, Italian name, they say, but that's not true. It's Levy. Anyway, she's given me over to the gendarmerie. They're not like the police. Darnand always said don't trust the gendarmes, they hate us, they turned their backs on the Maréchal from Day One.

Think of it. Back in those days, I could have had false emigration papers, straight from the Vatican, that Yugoslav bishop at the Holy See told Monsignor Le Moyne it would be no trouble at all. But I said no. I didn't want to be like Barbie in some South American backwater, peddling his arse as a secret policeman for a cheap little South American dictator, speaking Spanish, eating that greasy *métèque* food. I love France, it's my country, they're not going to drive me out of my own country. I'm French, I'll die in France!

Béziers. No one in the world knows I'm here tonight. Tomorrow I'll be in Aix. Maybe they'll know that. Maybe they'll send another Jew to kill me. How did they know I was in Salon? Who told them? Help me, God? Help me!

BÉZIERS. Next Exit.

CHAPTER EIGHT

César bounded up the steep flight of stairs, pulling her after him, straining on the lead as she fumbled for her keys. When she went into the apartment, her housekeeper, Madame Deferre, came out of the kitchen and whispered, 'Your visitor is here, Madame.'

She went into the sitting room, having first handed over César's lead. A young man stood up at once, with a slight, shy, bow.

'I'm Annemarie Livi. How do you do? Very good of you to come.'

They shook hands. 'I'm sorry I'm late,' she told him. 'I had to deliver my son to his school in Neuilly. There was some sort of delay on the Métro.'

'That's all right, Madame. I've just arrived.'

He was younger than she had imagined him to be, tall with reddish hair and a small, rather foolish moustache. She liked him at once.

'Professor, thank you very much for agreeing to see me. I read your dossier on Monsignor Le Moyne. I think it could be a great help to us. Would you like some coffee?'

'No, thank you.'

They sat down, facing each other. Suddenly, she felt no further need of formalities. 'Professor Valentin, first, let me say I know it's irregular, my asking to meet you. Tell me. The members of your commission, are they all historians?'

'Yes. Eight of us.'

'All laymen?'

'Except one. Monsignor Flandin. He's Secretary of the Ecclesiastical Committee for Relations with Judaism. He represents the Archbishop.'

'And when do you think you'll finish your investigation?'

'That's the problem, Madame. It may take a year or more.'

'Why so long?'

'We're trying to investigate forty years of delays and concealments. We're tracking down Brossard's contacts with all sorts of people in the Church. Even though there are eight of us, it's a slow process. And that's a pity. Because, in the meantime, the public is convinced that the Church is the only culprit in hiding him.'

She felt a small skip of excitement. But still, he's part of a Church commission. If he's working for the Cardinal, he'll try to shift the blame.

'So, you believe that Brossard may have other protectors?'

'Indeed, Madame. Powerful ones.'

'Government?'

'I'm guessing at all of this. I have no real proof. But I would say, possibly, the police up to the level of Prefect. Even the Elysée Palace seems to have been involved, under two different presidencies.'

'And what about your colleagues on the commission? Do they agree with you?'

'As far as I know, yes. We're each following different avenues of investigation, but in our first meetings we're very much agreed that there must have been other protectors. The trouble is, our commission was set up to investigate the Church's involvement and only that. My colleagues are not interested in pursuing these other links.'

'But you are?'

'I want *you* to pursue them, Madame. I don't have the means or the authority to do anything about it.'

'But may I be completely honest, Professor? Surely, it's in the Church's interest for your commission to exonerate these ecclesiastics who have helped Brossard over the years. And what better way than to shift part of the blame back to the civil

71

authority?'

She saw him stiffen in his chair. Then, surprisingly, he smiled. 'Of course. But let me tell you something, Madame. The members of our commission are historians, not Church apologists. Scholars like Professor Proulx or Dr Multon wouldn't have accepted this assignment if it were a cover-up. Besides, Madame, I feel that Cardinal Delavigne is sincere when he says he set up the investigation because he believes a wrong that is brought out into the open is preferable to a declaration of innocence, which is suspect.'

'I agree. The Cardinal's actions during the Occupation and afterwards show that he was totally anti-Nazi and on the side of the Resistance. But he's a son of the Church. And, as you know, the Vatican's record is murky in this regard. I'm talking of its attitude to the Germans during the war and immediately afterwards.'

'The post-war Vatican passports issued to Nazis to help them escape to South America?'

'Yes.'

'All true. But remember, the Church is not monolithic, particularly in France. Religious orders such as the Jesuits, the Dominicans, the Cistercians, et cetera, are a law unto themselves. Abbots and priors have a great deal of autonomy in their own monasteries. They can decide to help someone like Brossard, feeding him, lodging him and giving him money to live on, without having to ask permission, or even inform the local bishop or the hierarchy. In addition there's the medieval tradition of a churchly authority that puts itself above the laws of men. It's that sort of arrogance, I'm sure, that many of the priests who helped Brossard used to ease their conscience and flout the law. But in my researches, so far, I see no overall plan to hide Brossard. I mean, no plan coming down from the French hierarchy, let alone the Vatican.'

'But there's a plan somewhere. That's what interests me.'

He leaned forward in his chair, his face filled with conviction.

'Madame, that's what you must find out. Think of it. How did Brossard manage to escape from the hands of the police in the Rue des Saussaies back in 1945 when he was arrested and charged as a war criminal? How did he manage to stay in hiding from the late forties until now? The least one can say is that the police didn't search very diligently in order to find him. And how was it that in the sixties he managed to obtain a false identification card in the name of Pouliot, using as his address the address of the archbishopric in Lyon?'

'Is that true?'

'Yes. And, what's more, when it was discovered that the false address was the address of the archbishopric, the Prefect in Savoie received instructions from Paris to let the matter drop.'

'That could have been Church pressure.'

'Possibly. But then we come to the astonishing presidential pardon in 1971. If *Le Monde* hadn't got wind of it and broken the story, Brossard would be a free man today, a small fish, forgotten. And so, this new charge of a crime against humanity might never have come up. It's this charge which for the first time is being levelled at Frenchmen, not Germans, that's worrying certain people. You know who I'm talking about. Three other Frenchmen are similarly charged but have never been brought to trial. But if Brossard is caught and tried, their trials can't be put off any longer. So, to sum up, Madame, I don't believe that the Church alone had the power to help Brossard escape the police and the courts over a forty-year period.'

'But the public believes it.'

'Yes. And unless we find Brossard, they'll continue to believe it. And that simplification of events, that falsification of the truth, will become a part of French history.'

'And will that be so terrible, Professor? I mean, to those of us who are not historians?'

'The study of history is not so different from the practice of the law, Madame. The primary aim of both is to discover the truth of events, isn't it?'

'Mine was a foolish remark,' she said. 'I'm sorry. Of course, I agree with you. And it's only now, in 1989, that little judges like me have come to realize that we can indict the Establishment. One thing puzzles me in all of this. If you believe that the Church isn't Brossard's only protector, why did you send me the Le Moyne dossier?'

'Because the Church is still hiding him. So you've got to find him through that network of concealment. I sent it because I noticed something in it which may be the key to tracking Brossard down. The Chevaliers.'

'Sorry?'

'In some of the letters written by Monsignor Le Moyne, there's mention of a group of right-wing Catholic activists called the Chevaliers de Ste Marie. In one letter, which I marked, Le Moyne says Brossard was made a Chevalier in this Order and that the Order is helping him financially.'

'I see. Do you know Colonel Roux?'

'No.'

'He's conducting the investigation. I'll contact him at once.'

'Good.'

The telephone rang in the hall. She heard Madame Deferre go to answer it. At once, the young man stood up. 'I must leave now, Madame.'

'No, no, please.' She stood up. 'I won't be a moment.'

He held out his hand. 'I really must.'

'Telephone, Madame.'

'One moment.' She led him to the door. César bounded out of the kitchen, tail wagging. The young man patted the dog's head and said, 'The Chevaliers aren't a schismatic group. But they have links to those traditionalist priests who have recently broken with Rome. To the former Archbishop of Dakar.'

César. She had to reach down and grip the dog's collar to prevent him following the young man out of the door. 'Dakar?' she said. 'Monsignor Lefebvre?'

He nodded. 'Goodbye, Madame.'

CHAPTER NINE

The residence was separated from the school by a narrow alleyway. The homeless, most of them alcoholics, would drift into the alley shortly before noon at a time when the schoolboys were playing noisily in the adjoining school yard. Soup was distributed to these men at twelve-thirty. Father Blaise, the *père hospitalier*, usually unlocked the back door himself and supervised the distribution which was carried out by two of the lay brothers. That particular morning, with the noise from the school yard, the bell, ringing repeatedly, was not at first noticed by the brothers in the kitchen. But when Father Blaise came out of his office he heard it.

'Who's ringing the bell? Is it one of the *clochards*?'

'There's a young fellow who's been hanging round for the past few days,' Brother André said. 'He's off his head. I bet it's him.'

Father Blaise took out his keys and went through the scullery to the back door. A table was set up there with soup bowls, spoons and a basket full of bread. He unlocked the door expecting to deal with some drunken derelict. But instead there was an elderly man in a green woollen cardigan, corduroy trousers, a respectable type, not the usual figure in the soup line. The *clochards*, sitting along the alley wall, began to get to their feet when they saw that the door had been opened.

'Did you ring the bell?' Father Blaise asked the old man.

'Yes, Father. Good morning. Is Father Dominic here?'

'I'm afraid Father Dominic has passed away.'

'I am so sorry. God rest his soul. Are you the new *père hospitalier*?'

'I am, yes.'

'I am Pierre Pouliot. I'm a friend of the Abbot. Is he in?'

Father Blaise looked again at the old man. He felt a sense of shock. It must be him. The photograph is in my office.

'The Abbot is over at the school at present,' he said. 'I'm expecting him back here shortly. If you'd like to come in and wait, I'll see if I can find him.'

The homeless were now crowding up to the door.

76

Two of the brothers came out of the kitchen, carrying between them a huge iron bowl filled with soup. Father Blaise pushed aside the serving table to let the old man enter. As the brothers began to serve the soup, Father Blaise led the old man through the residence and put him into the front parlour.

'It may take a while,' he said. 'If you'll please wait?'

'No hurry, no hurry,' the old man said, seating himself comfortably in a chair near the window. 'Thank you very much, Father.'

Blaise went at once to his office. In a drawer where correspondence was kept he found and examined the photograph that had been given to him a week ago. Two priests from the diocesan office had come one morning when the Abbot was away. They had come, they said, with instructions from the Bishop who, in turn, had received instructions from Cardinal Delavigne, the Primate, in Lyon. They had shown him this photograph and asked if he knew this man. He did not.

'Well, he's a regular visitor to this house. We know that. He has been for a number of years.'

'I'm new here. I was transferred from St Sauveur, the month before last.'

'Perhaps that explains it,' the visiting priest said. 'I'm going to give you this photograph. It was taken only seven years ago, so you should be able to recognize him. We're distributing it everywhere he was admitted or may have been admitted in the past.'

He looked at the photograph. Two old men standing in a garden. One of them was a cleric. The other was the old man, now in the parlour.

'The man on the right is Pierre Brossard. Are you allowed to read newspapers and watch television in this house?'

'Not in this house, no. The Abbot does not permit television or any form of press. But when I was at St Sauveur, it was different. So I know who he is. The *milicien*.'

'That's right. Do you know that the Church has come under criticism for sheltering him?'

'Yes. We were told that, when I was at St Sauveur.'

'Good. The reason we're here is because Cardinal Delavigne has given strict instructions that, from now on, Brossard is to be turned away at once from any church property where he tries to gain asylum. There are to be no exceptions. We know that in several of the places he has been sheltered his identity has been revealed only to the Abbot and the *père hospitalier*. Would that be the case here?'

'I would think so, yes. In our Order, the *hospitalier* is the only one to know a visitor's name. Apart, of course, from the Abbot himself.'

'In that case, as the Abbot is not here today, we'll leave it to you to tell him about this matter. If he has any further questions about it, please ask him to get in touch with the Cardinal directly.'

When the Abbot returned that evening, Blaise showed him the photograph.

'That's Maurice Le Moyne,' the Abbot said.

'I'm sorry. Who?'

'The priest with him is Monsignor Le Moyne. He's been a great champion of Pierre Brossard's case. The whole thing is disgusting.'

'I'm sorry, Father Abbot. I don't think I understand.'

'Pierre is one of us. It's terrible to let him down now. Delavigne's a leftist, of course, afraid of the press and the Jewish lobby. He doesn't have the guts to stand his ground.'

'But Brossard was a war criminal, wasn't he? There's no doubt about that?'

The Abbot was caught in a fit of coughing, a legacy of his malaria from the Southern African years. When the coughing had subsided, he put his hand on Blaise's shoulder and said, in a kindly tone, 'Father, I don't know you very well, but I am sure your heart is in the right place. I am an old man now and I find it hard to renounce the things I have always believed in. One of the things I will always believe is that we lost the war, not in 1940, but in 1945.'

'Did you say '45, Father Abbot?'

'Yes. Let me explain. In 1940, under Maréchal Pétain, France was given a chance to revoke the errors, the weakness and selfishness, of the Third Republic, that regime that caused us to lose the war to the Germans. Of course, it was a sad time. I'm not denying it. Part of the country was occupied, but you must remember there *was* a large free zone, the zone of the Vichy Government, the Maréchal's government, which was giving us the hope of a new co-operation between our country and Germany. Under the Maréchal, we were led away from selfish materialism and those democratic parliaments that preached a false equality back to the Catholic values we were brought up in: the family, the nation, the Church. But when the Germans lost the war, all that was finished. Stalin's communist armies overran Europe. The enemies of religion came back in force. I believe that poor Pierre Brossard wasn't very different from me, or from many others. He was brought up to believe the things we believed in, he fought for those things, he was loyal, as most Frenchmen were, not to de Gaulle, far away in London with the English who deserted us in 1940,

79

but to the Maréchal who did not run away but stayed to unite us. Unfortunately, Brossard eventually chose to join the *milice*, which, I agree, became brutal in the end. But I also believe in forgiveness, Father. I believe in contrition. I believe that Pierre Brossard was led into error but has since repented for his sins and, like hundreds of others who lived through those times, is being victimized for fighting and believing in values that were anathema to the communists who controlled the Resistance. And so I think it's a disgrace that now, in his hour of greatest need, the main body of the Church shows him no mercy and sends these priests around with orders that we are to shut him out.'

'But, Father Abbot, the beliefs of the *milice* were the beliefs of the Nazis. And the Nazis were certainly not Catholic. Besides, Brossard didn't need orders from the Nazis. He was always a step ahead of them. From what I've read it's clear that he carried out the assassination of those fourteen Jews in Dombey. He stole Jewish property, et cetera, et cetera. And, if what I was taught in the seminary is still the rule, Father, the Church, while it aids those who are persecuted, does not shelter proven criminals fleeing from justice.'

'The Church is not bound by man's laws, but by the law of God,' the Abbot said. 'Judgements handed down by the State don't necessarily absolve us, as Christians, from helping unfortunates who seek our help.'

'Does that mean that if Brossard arrives on our doorstep I am to admit him?'

'He won't show up,' the Abbot said. 'He visits us very infrequently. But if he does, yes, admit him. I will speak to him. And having spoken to him, I will

80

act according to my conscience.'

And now, a week later, Brossard was sitting in the parlour. Blaise put the photograph back in the drawer and went out, crossing the avenue to the main gates of the school. The Abbot was in the school office, eating a bowl of the same soup that was being served to the *clochards* in the alley.

'Brossard? You're sure it's Brossard?'

'I can't be sure, Father Abbot. But he looks like the man in that photograph. He said his name was Pouliot.'

'That's him. Where is he now?'

'I put him in the parlour. What shall I do? Do you want me to admit him?'

The Abbot rose, stepping out from behind his desk. 'Did he ask for a room?'

'No, Father.'

'Good. I have to talk to him. I'll let you know.'

Let me know what? Is he going to turn him away after all? I doubt it. What *is* the rule of obedience? To obey one's superior in the Order? Yes, of course. But is there a higher rule, the rule of obedience to the Cardinal Primate, the leader of the Church in France? If the Abbot shelters this Nazi turd, isn't it my duty to report it?

CHAPTER TEN

For as long as he could remember, he had held older men in respect. It went back to his father Henri Brossard, an old army man, ever the drill sergeant barking out commands, a ruler up his back, a parade-ground walk. His father had, in turn, looked up to the

81

greatest of old men. The Maréchal. His father had served under the Maréchal in the First World War. The Maréchal was France. Religion also spoke in the tones of age. It was ancient and all powerful. It must be obeyed. The Pope was the Holy Father. But now that he himself was old, he no longer saw older men in a respectful light. Now, he looked at them for signs of failure: the faltering step on the stairs, the voice hesitating over a forgotten surname, the look of quiet deception when dimming ears had missed what was said. Now he measured them and their frailties against his own. And judged himself the victor.

He had known Dom André Vergnes for twenty years. At first, he had been intimidated by the Abbot's manner and voice: the voice of Paris's great schools, the accent he thought of and feared as *snob*. But, as always with clerics, he knew, at once, when he was likely to be believed and what would appeal to his listener. He could tell a priest's politics in something so slight as a nod or a smile. The hesitation of the Jew lover when you brought the Yids into your tale. The sudden second look when you mentioned the *milice*. He knew, at once, whether a priest or monk had read the papers and followed cases such as his. He knew when a simple *curé* would give him a night's lodging out of Christian charity without caring who or what he was. He knew the group who could be told part of his tale, who, while they might despise his past and condemn his actions, could be won by his penitence, and trusted, through the imperative of confession, to protect him from the laws of men. He also knew the group who could be told the truth, or most of it, who, while not sure of his total innocence, were sympathetic, hostile to this leftist, godless France. And then, of course, there

82

were what he called the true believers: a small group, now growing smaller, those who had remained faithful when the wind had changed, who saw the long years of protecting him as their duty, a proof that, in backing Vichy, they themselves had made the proper choice.

Dom André was seventy-nine, almost a decade older than he. In the ninth decade, as he well knew, men become stubborn and unyielding, unwilling to admit error now that judgement day is close. Because of this he had little fear that Dom André would be swayed by Cardinal Delavigne's order. But you never know. And so, when Dom André came into the parlour, he rose up to greet him, but deferentially, cautiously, waiting to see how the wind blew.

'Ah, Pierre. How are you?'

A handshake. It told him nothing.

'I can't complain. And yourself, Father Abbot? How have you been?'

The Abbot sat stiffly in a chair by the parlour table, resting his elbows on the table, lowering his head slightly. A sign of dizziness?

'I am well,' the Abbot said. 'I hear you've been moving about?'

What does he mean by that?

'Yes. The usual. Can't be too careful, particularly now.'

'You've been in Salon,' the Abbot said. 'I know, because I had a telephone call from my old friend Dom Vladimir, the night before last. He asked me if I'd seen or heard of you.'

'I wonder why, Father Abbot?'

'Well, he said that in the past you've often come on here, after staying for a few weeks at St Cros.'

'That's true.'

83

'He seemed quite worried. He warned me that you might be in serious trouble.'

'Trouble, Father Abbot? Nothing new about that, is there?'

'I'm afraid this *is* new, Pierre. Apparently, the day after you left St Cros, Dom Vladimir had a visit from the police. They'd found a car and a body in a ravine, just a few miles down the road. As you know, that road leads only to the abbey and to a few farmhouses. So they wanted to know if Dom Vladimir knew this person who'd been killed. There were no papers on the body, but it was identified through the car-rental people in Marseille. The driver was a Canadian, called Tanenbaum. Dom Vladimir had never heard of him.'

'But why *should* he know anything about it? It was probably an ordinary accident.'

He saw the Abbot hesitate. That was well put. Just what I would say if I knew nothing.

'Not exactly. The man had been shot in the chest. It could have been a simple robbery and murder. But Dom Vladimir was struck by the fact that this must have happened just a few hours before you suddenly informed him that you were leaving St Cros that same evening.'

'Pure coincidence, Father Abbot. These days I can't afford to stay long in any one place. But one thing puzzles me. How could Dom Vladimir think I had anything to do with this man's death?'

'I'm not able to speak for him, Pierre. But he did point out that Tanenbaum is a Jewish name.'

'Tanenbaum? Who? Oh, yes, the man who was shot.'

'Pierre, we all know that the Jews are the ones who are seeking revenge. Look, I'm not accusing you of killing this man. But, as Dom Vladimir pointed out, you might have been forced to defend yourself.'

'Father, I've the greatest respect for Dom Vladimir. I revere him. But, if I may say so, perhaps he has been reading too many detective stories lately.'

He kept a smile on his face as he said this. And at the same time stared directly into the Abbot's eyes. He'll believe me. It's too Grand Guignol for him to believe otherwise.

But the Abbot did a worrying thing. He rose from his chair and went to look out of the window at the school across the road. The lunchtime break was ending. An electric bell shrilled, calling the boys back to lessons. The Abbot did not turn round. He spoke in a quiet, careful tone.

'Pierre, this is a difficult time for all of us. You know about the Cardinal's commission?'

'Yes, Father Abbot.'

'And did you know our Bishop has been sending two priests around with a copy of your photograph and instructions that we are not to admit you if you ask for asylum?'

'No, I didn't, Father Abbot. Of course, I wouldn't have embarrassed you, if I'd known that was the case.'

'Wait. I didn't mean it that way. If I hadn't had this call from Dom Vladimir, I'd have ignored the Cardinal's order. I am an independent prelate and I don't have to obey the archbishopric. But now, I don't know what to think. You may have wanted to spare Dom Vladimir any involvement in this matter. As you may want to spare me. But I think, for all our sakes, that I need to know the truth. Of course, under no circumstances will it go further than this room. You have my word on that.'

85

'And you have my word, Father. I've never heard of Monsieur Tanenbaum. I've never set eyes on him.'

'Well, that *is* good news,' the Abbot said. But he kept staring out of the window.

He doesn't believe me.

And then the Abbot said, 'Pierre, I feel badly about this, but I must think of the school, the parents, and our duty to avoid any scandal at this juncture. As you know, I've always supported you and I'd be happy to keep you here, just as in the old days. But I'm worried. Some of our monks might not agree with me. And with all the publicity you've received, I can no longer be sure that, if you stay here, they will remain ignorant of your identity. Therefore, I don't feel I can offer you a bed, not even for tonight. However, I'll be happy to help you financially if you can find a *pension* or somewhere to stay for the period you might have spent with us.'

Now, at last, the Abbot turned round to face him. It had been said. One could always tell when the tide had turned, when, in fact, it was dangerous to say or do anything that let them know you knew they had changed sides.

He got up at once. 'Father Abbot, thank you. God bless you. I'd ask one favour. Pray for me. I need your prayers now, more than ever.'

'Of course I will,' the Abbot said. 'And money?'

'No, no, I'll be all right.'

'Will you be able to find somewhere to stay in Aix?'

'I think I'll move on. And, please, Father, if you're speaking to Dom Vladimir, I'd be grateful if you would reassure him about that man's death.'

'Yes, of course I will.'

They went out of the parlour and down the hall to the front entrance. As they did, they passed the little office of the *père hospitalier*. He saw the new *hospitalier*, Father Blaise, look up from his desk.

He knows who I am.

The Abbot opened the heavy front door and, as so often in the past, clasped him briefly in a farewell embrace. 'Safe journey, Pierre.'

The Judas kiss.

* * *

Dom André watched Pierre Brossard walk off down the Avenue Henri Martin, his step brisk, his head upright. He watched him turn the corner of the street and disappear. Will I ever see him again? Will he be captured at last, brought into the light of day, cameras, reporters, lawyers, judges, editorials in *Le Monde*? Or will he stay in darkness until the hour of his death?

These thoughts ran through his brain like sentences in a conversation with someone else and then, as he feared, deserted him, leaving in their place the shame of knowing he had sent Brossard away, not from principle, but in cowardice. In these last years it had not been difficult to give shelter to a man who, in his youth, had committed acts of violence, who had, in all probability, killed his enemies. Because that was wartime, the Occupation, a time forgotten by many and unknown to the young. Even he who had lived through those years now saw them as faded and dim, a half-remembered book read long ago.

But hearing Vladimir on the telephone from Salon the night before last, everything we did, our prayers for God's mercy in this case, the letters we wrote in support of Maurice Le Moyne's appeals, the money I took from our community fund to help support Brossard in those early years of clandestineness, what if, in helping him, we were not doing the work of Christian charity, but simply protecting someone whose ideas in the years of Occupation were close to our own? I, in particular, believed him, I knelt beside him in our chapel and prayed for his salvation. I felt the glow of righteousness, of helping a sinner find God's grace, of acting as mentor to a man who had become a devout Catholic, a victim of that madness we lived through when the war ended and the French people, filled with hatred, sought to purge themselves of guilt by making scapegoats of a few. I had believed in the Maréchal, that fine old soldier brought down by de Gaulle, a preening egoist the Maréchal once treated as a son. I was bitter and that bitterness I now see was the truth behind my actions, perhaps behind all of our actions in the years we sheltered Brossard.

Half an hour ago, I looked out of the window, his voice at my back, familiar, devotional, sincere. And, suddenly, for the first time, I knew he was lying. God knows what dupes he's made of us. He's a scoundrel. I know it. He's the father of lies. If he killed that Jew in self-defence and told me honestly that he had done it, I'd have been sick, I'd have been afraid to have him under my roof, but I would have sheltered him.

Or would I?

I don't know. I've lost faith in myself. I call Brossard a scoundrel and a liar, but am I not a liar myself? Do any of us know the hidden motives behind our actions, especially those of us who pray nightly to God to forgive us our sins, yet all the time pride ourselves on being better than others, not evil, not fornicators, criminals, or men of deception in our daily lives. Easy to believe these things when God has not tested us. As today, I was tested by Brossard. Be honest. If he had told me the truth, wouldn't I have got rid of him?

Of course I would. How can I pretend otherwise? I want nothing more to do with him. He deserves to be caught.

Dom André closed the front door of the residence and walked back down the corridor. Father Blaise came out of his office, his face greedy for news. 'So, Father Abbot. Will our friend be back?'

'No. I sent him away.'

Dom André walked on, going up the staircase to the privacy of his office. He rang the St Cros number.

'Vladimir. He came here this morning. I told him what you told me. He says he's never heard of the man. He wanted me to reassure you. But, Vladimir, I have to tell you. I did not believe him.'

'Where is he now?'

'I sent him away.'

'That was wise, André. I haven't told you of the latest development. First, this was a story in the newspapers about a foreign tourist being robbed and killed. But today there's a new story in *Nice-Matin*. Apparently, the Canadian authorities have checked the dead man's driving licence and found it to be false. Yesterday, the police came back to ask me if I was expecting any visitor by another name. Of course, I said no. But André, I am like you. I have a bad feeling about this. As I told you before, the name on the licence was Tanenbaum. A Jewish name.'

'Wait a minute. If the licence was false, the name on it could also be false.'

'True. But Pierre wouldn't know that, would he? If he thought the man was a Jew trying to murder him, what do you think an ex-*milicien* would do? Kill him.

89

Take his money. Hide the papers. Make it look like murder for money.'

'Oh my God. It's possible, I suppose.'

'It's more than possible. André, I've changed my mind about this. I think we should tell the archbishopric that Brossard has been staying with me in St Cros, and that he came seeking asylum at your residence today.'

'No. We can't do that.'

'Why not?'

'What if the Cardinal contacts the police? The police will come to see us. The press will get hold of the story. We and our communities will be pilloried as his accomplices.'

There was a silence on the line to St Cros.

'Vladimir?'

'André, I don't think the Cardinal will contact the police. He has said publicly that the role of his commission is to investigate the Church's involvement, not to act as policemen in hunting down Brossard.'

'But he may feel obliged to do it.'

'That decision is his to make. Not ours.'

'Vladimir, if the police find Pierre, *we* will be the ones who are responsible. Do we want to have it on our conscience that he'll be locked up in prison for the rest of his life?'

Again, there was silence on the line to St Cros.

'Vladimir?'

'Do we want to have it on our conscience that a man was murdered, that we may have helped the murderer escape and that a week from now, he may kill again? André, I'll leave you out of it, if you like. But I must speak to Delavigne.'

'No. You're right. It's time to tell the truth.'

*　　*　　*

On the night of May the 5th, T, arriving from Paris, booked into a Novotel near the airport. Next morning he drove into the suburbs of Aix, well before the rush hour. Brossard was due in Aix on May the 6th. At 8.30 a.m. T parked his rented car at the corner of the Avenue Henri Martin and the Avenue Paul Valéry, one street away from the Lycée St Christophe and the priory that was on the opposite side of the street from the school. Boys with satchels were being let out of cars by their parents. At eight-forty-five when the school bell started ringing T got out of his rented car and walked up to the school entrance as the last stragglers ran past him, hurrying to get in before the bell stopped.

There were no cars parked in the school yard. He crossed the street and looked through the iron railings at the front of the priory. Three cars were parked at the main entrance. No white Peugeot. He walked down the street and saw that there were *No Parking* signs on both the Avenue Henri Martin and the Avenue Paul Valéry. Perhaps the monks had a garage in the rear of the priory? T went to look. The rear entrance to the priory was connected to the street by an alley, too narrow to accommodate a car. The alley was a cul-de-sac.

No white Peugeot anywhere. T went back to the Avenue Henri Martin. At the far end of the Avenue he found a small square. The name of the café on the corner of this square was Café La Mascotte. He looked at the name of the square. Place des Tanneurs. The names matched the note he had been given. So the old fart didn't go into town in the afternoons. He hung out at this corner café. That could make

91

things easy.

Waiting was part of the job. Sitting on your arse, hour after hour, keeping your eyes open. He sometimes played tapes, American rock. French rock was shit. Pochon had told the Jews that the rented car must be big enough to look like a limo. T wore a dark suit and a chauffeur's cap. That way, people didn't find it funny, you sitting there hour after hour. It was part of your job.

The school bell was electric and rang every forty minutes, when classes changed. It got on his nerves. A little after 11 a.m. four *clochards* came staggering up the avenue. They stopped, refreshed themselves from a bottle of *gros rouge*, then walked out into the street in front of his car and began muttering some drunken shit about capitalists. One of them kicked his front tyre. T rolled down the window, smiled at them and said, 'What can I do? It's a job.' It worked. One of them wiped the neck of the bottle and offered him a swig. He pretended to drink, then passed it back. They staggered on, going into the alley. He saw them sit down on the cobblestones near the rear entrance to the priory. By noon, they had been joined by eight other *clochards*, two of them women. He watched each group as it went in and then, just to make sure, got out of the car, lit a cigarette and walked up the alley, passing the priory's back door. The door was open now and two monks were serving soup to the *clochards* from a table placed across the entrance. The *clochards* formed a line at the open door, like people queuing for tables at a posh restaurant. They seemed to be regulars. They knew each other. No sign of the subject. T went back to his car.

At one o'clock that afternoon T went down to the

café on the corner and ate a sandwich. He positioned himself so that he could watch the front entrance as he ate. He could also see the entrance to the rear alley. No sign of the subject.

At four o'clock, his arse sore, he got out of the car again and went back to the café. He found the phone booth, telephoned Janine, got her machine and left a message, saying that his father was a bit better and he would call later. He said it was pouring with rain, here in Bayeux.

As the afternoon wore into evening, he walked up and down the street a few times. He was now sure it wouldn't be today. Still, he waited until most of the lights had gone out in the priory before driving back to the Novotel Hotel. He ate fast food in a McDo, set his alarm for seven and tried to sleep. Something wasn't right. They'd said that Brossard would arrive in Aix on the 6th. What if he doesn't turn up tomorrow or the next day? Then we'll be at the 9th. The horoscope said, 'On the 9th you will be forced into an action that could do you great harm.' Shit, he knew the horoscope had been cooked up by some cunt in an office. But that didn't help. He was afraid of horoscopes. In the past, they had come true.

On the morning of the 7th he again arrived at the Avenue Henri Martin at eight-thirty, watched the school's pupils go in at eight-forty-five, and checked both courtyards. No white Peugeot. By 11 a.m. the first *clochards* had arrived and were sitting on their arses in the back alley. The second day of a stakeout was always more boring than the first. In a place like this, a suburb, one day was just like another. You saw the same people on the streets. At noon, the school bell rang for break and he heard boys shouting as they ran into the yard. Two monks came out of the priory carrying a big soup bowl and a basket of bread. They crossed the street and went into the school. T felt he needed to take a piss. He got out and walked up the back alley just as the monks opened the rear door for the *clochards'* soup. Just as he was zipping up his trousers he saw one of the monks pull aside the table that blocked the rear entrance. An old, white-headed *clochard*, wearing a green cardigan, was allowed into the kitchen and then the monks pulled the table back in place and went on serving soup. T watched for ten minutes. The old man didn't come out again. He hadn't seen the old man's face.

T went back to the car. He saw a monk leave the priory and walk across the street to the school. After a few minutes, the same monk came out of the school with a second monk, a tall old grey-beard wearing a crucifix on a chain around his neck. The head monk? They crossed the street and went into the priory. Why did they let that old guy into the kitchen? T took out the two photographs and studied them. He checked his gun and slipped it into a shoulder holster. He did not have a plan. Not yet. If the old man came out of either entrance, he'd have to walk to the place where he'd left his car. Or to a taxi rank. The nearest taxi rank was on the Place des Tanneurs. T did not believe in improv, but you had to be flexible. Once he had a subject in his sights, he knew how to be patient. If this *was* the subject?

Ten minutes later, the front door of the priory opened and he saw the white-headed old man come out on to the front steps. The tall, grey-bearded monk came out with him, embraced him and stood watching as the old man walked across the courtyard, opened the front gate and came out on to the Avenue Henri Martin. T put the Renault in gear.

94

The old man walked off in the direction of the Place des Tanneurs. T drove slowly past him, studying him through the side mirror. Brossard? He couldn't be sure.

CHAPTER ELEVEN

'Safe journey, Pierre,' he says as he gives me the Judas kiss, his arms around me on the steps of the Prieuré St Christophe. St Christophe, the patron saint of travellers. Did he see the irony of turning me away at St Christophe's door? He offers me money but denies me shelter. As I walk away now, I know he's watching, waiting to see how I take his betrayal. Step out like a soldier. Left, Right, Left, Right! When it's over, it's over. Thank you, Dom André.

And thank you, Dom Vladimir at Salon, phoning ahead to make sure I'm not welcome. Will he phone Villefranche? He might. Once your luck turns, the roulette wheel spins, the ball falls into losing slots. What will I do now, will I go directly to Villefranche?

He was walking down towards the Place des Tanneurs. His old café, La Mascotte, was on the corner. His car was in the municipal car-park three streets away. He could telephone from La Mascotte. And eat something. He remembered they had a good *salade niçoise* at La Mascotte. He was hungry. He'd planned his arrival at the priory to coincide with the lunch hour, coming in at the back door when the *père hospitalier* would be supervising the serving of soup to the *clochards*. Usually, if he did this, Dominic would ask him if he had eaten yet. But Dominic is dead, the new man said.

A car, a big Renault limousine with chauffeur, drove slowly past him, going down towards the Place des Tanneurs. He looked at the back seat. No passenger. The Renault was crawling along at 20 kilometres an hour, as if the driver was searching for a street address. But then he saw that the driver wasn't looking at the numbers on the buildings, he was peering into his side-view mirror. The steel ball in the roulette wheel dropped into the bad-luck slot. He's looking at *me*.

When you picked up a tail the important thing was to make sure they didn't know about it. He walked on at the same pace, ignoring the Renault, which now speeded up a little, entering the square before him. La Mascotte was busy. There were no tables free. Monsieur Pierre went to the bar, ordered a *bière pression* and sat on a stool looking out at the square. He saw the Renault circle the square and come back slowly past the café. He didn't think the driver could see him. He watched the Renault circle the square once again and park two streets away from where he was sitting. The driver got out, lit a cigarette and walked slowly towards La Mascotte. This time, the driver saw him sitting at the counter. The driver turned and went back to his car.

At once, Monsieur Pierre put down money for his drink, walked past the toilets and through the kitchen. Nobody paid him any attention. He came out into the lane behind the café, not knowing where he was. The lane was long. At the end of it, he came to a main thoroughfare, the Rue Renaud. He found a taxi rank and took a taxi to the municipal *parking* on Avenue Goncourt where his little Peugeot was parked. He was out of breath as he hurried across the car-park and settled into the driver's seat. He took his

96

pulse, shut his eyes and tried to empty his mind. It was an old trick, learned long ago when he was the hunter, not the hunted, a form of empty meditation in which he recited, over and over again, the first nonsense syllables that came into his head. Today it was:

Minute Papillon!
Minute Papillon!
Minute Papillon!
Minute Papillon!

His lips moved in a whisper, like a child learning to speak. He felt his mind go blank. He sat in the little car, his head bowed. Think. Put yourself in their shoes. These Yids, whoever they are, knew when I'd be in Salon and where to find me. I don't think they followed me to Caunes. No, but they were expecting me here in Aix. They knew I would go to the priory. They staked me out there. If they know that, they know that on my usual route I'll go from Aix to Villefranche.

Someone is giving me to them. Someone who knows my moves.

Hide. Move off the track. Nicole? No one knows about her. No one.

Nicole. He put the car in gear.

CHAPTER TWELVE

He saw the old man at the bar, saw him with a glass in his hand. He might eat at the bar. Afterwards, would he go back to the monks' house? T walked back to his car and moved it closer to the Café La Mascotte. He lit another cigarette. The horoscope, he could not forget that fucking horoscope. 'On the 9th . . .' OK, that's tomorrow. I'd better do it today. White Peugeot. He's parked somewhere around here. Follow him when he comes out of the café. I could do it in the car-park, do it as he goes to get his car. If he falls between parked cars he might not be seen for a while. Anyway, relax. You have him in place. Stay in the car. The old paper-shuffler's a professional. If you walk past the café a second time, he might notice you.

But twenty minutes later he had a gut feeling that he'd better check again. He got out and walked past the café. The subject wasn't in sight. He went into the café. No sign of the old man. He went into the toilet, a risky move. No sign. Back entrance, a long alley leading to a main street. Gone. He saw me.

Or did he? If he did, he'll not go back to the school, he'll find his car and disappear. Leave Aix. Pochon: 'If for any reason you lose him, phone me at once. At once, do you hear!'

T drove back up the Avenue Henri Martin and parked at the same place as before, a street away from the school and the monks' residence. He sat there all afternoon. Sat there because there was nothing else he could hope for but that the old man would pick up his car and come back to spend the night. But he knew. He knew. If he didn't see me, why did he go out the back way?

And the tall monk. When they hugged each other, they were saying goodbye. He'll not be back.

'If for any reason you lose him, phone me at once, do you hear?'

At seven o'clock that evening he drove back to the
98

Novotel Hotel at the airport, went into his room and picked up the phone. Shit! And it isn't even the 9th.

CHAPTER THIRTEEN

'Do you know what he thinks—he thinks if he gets us to do the room in twelve minutes he can go back to the big American boss and tell him he only needs sixteen chambermaids and not twenty-two. That's what Yvette says. And she's right.'

'Yvette is a communist,' Madame Maranne said. 'I can do a room in twelve minutes, if I have to. If we don't do it, they'll bring in foreigners.'

'Strip the bed, change the sheets, clean the toilet and washbowl in the bathroom, wet-mop the bathroom floor, put out fresh towels and soaps, dust the lamps and tables, vacuum the carpets. Twelve minutes! Room after room. At our age, that's not work, it's the gulag.'

They were riding the municipal bus, going home to Cannes from their jobs as chambermaids in the Majestic Hotel in La Napoule. The Majestic, taken over six months ago by an American syndicate, had been turned into a casino hotel with roulette and blackjack, and one-arm bandits in the lobby. A new pool had been installed. The public rooms had been re-furbished. Madame Maranne, who had worked in the old Majestic for seventeen years, had received a small rise in pay, a week after the Americans took over. In her opinion, Madame Dufy was talking out of turn. If the Americans wanted the rooms done in twelve minutes, then you vacuumed every second day. Nobody needed to know. Just keep your eyes open for dirt on the floor. But she held her tongue. Madame Dufy was a talker. Like Yvette. The Americans didn't care who did the work. If you complained to the Americans, *noirs* and *beurs* would get your job.

The bus was coming into Cannes. Madame Maranne's stop was at the Quai St Pierre. When she got up from her seat, a little package of ground beef she'd bought for Bobi spilled out of her shopping bag and fell under the seat. She didn't notice it but Madame Dufy did. Dufy, who was twenty years younger than she, got down on her knees to pry it out. The bus driver held the door for her. She and Madame Dufy shook hands as usual. 'Till tomorrow, then. And thank you, eh?'

Not a bad soul, Madame Dufy, when all was said and done. Madame Maranne set off down Rue Louis Le Blanc, thinking how upset she'd have been if she'd got home and had no treat for Bobi. Bobi was uncanny. That dog knew as well as any human being that this was Friday, it was pay day, it was the day for his treat. What do we know about animals? They're God's creatures, the same as us, I said to Mother Annunciata, I said you can't tell me Bobi's just going to die but that I'm going to die and go to Heaven. Animals have no soul, she said. If you think otherwise you're going against the teachings of your religion. Nuns knew nothing about anything, certainly not about real life, and maybe not even about religion. Just because Mother Annunciata was Reverend Mother over thirty odd nuns didn't mean she had the right to say that about Bobi. Had God given her some special knowledge, Mother Annunciata? Nuns and their notions! To think that long ago she herself had wanted to take the veil, become a nun, shut herself away from the world. Not that the world had treated her so well. No, indeed. But Bobi, I was thinking of Bobi. No human being is capable of the love Bobi has for me. No one.

*   *   *

At the far end of the Rue Louis Le Blanc, she waited for the Number 86 bus. Her apartment on Rue Cochet was on the ground floor, and very dark but, now that Bobi was blind, to be on the ground floor was a blessing. Bobi was an Alsatian, and because he could no longer see the stairs she would have had to carry him up and down. For he still liked his walk. Not just to do *pipi* and his business, but he became excited as a puppy once he smelled the open air. And she, well the truth was, the only time she forgot her age and felt young again was when Bobi started pulling at the lead as they came into the park at the Place de Gaulle.

When Madame Maranne got out her key and put it in the apartment door she listened for the usual bark. Instead, a man's voice asked, 'Who is it?'

She had a moment of panic, then thought of the concierge. 'Is that you, Monsieur Delisle?' Delisle was the husband of Madame Delisle, the concierge. He had been working on the ball and chain of the toilet.

She heard the door unlock. The door opened. It was not Monsieur Delisle. It was *him*. She pushed past him. 'Bobi? Bobi, where are you?'

'I shut him up in the kitchen,' he said.

'Shit!' She turned to him as if she would slap him, then went to the kitchen and opened the door. Poor Bobi clambered up on her skirt, licking her hand.

'There, Bobi, there Bobi,' she said. 'I have something nice for you, don't you worry.'

He came into the kitchen behind her as she took down Bobi's bowl and mixed up the ground meat with a fork.

'I have something nice for *you*,' he said.

She paid him no heed. What was he doing here? What did he want, he wanted something, you could bet on that, it was always the same with him. It was over a year since he'd been back to pester her. In the old days he came for sex, but now he was getting too old for it, they both were. She hunkered down to watch Bobi eat his treat. 'Good Bobi, good baby. You like that, don't you?'

That dog, I tell you, there was never another animal like him. Imagine, hungry as he was, Bobi stopped eating, looked up at her with his poor eyes, white with glaucoma, and reached his head forward, sniffing her arm, then licking it before he went back to his treat. The other one came around behind Bobi, fanning out in his hand, like a pack of cards, a fistful of 500-franc notes. 'Where did you get that?' she said.

'From a dead Yid. I'm superstitious. It wouldn't be lucky for me to spend Jew money just now. So I decided I'd make you a nice present.'

She looked at the money in his hand, then looked away. There must be 5,000 francs there, maybe more. I said a long time ago that I'd not take another penny from him, even though there's no reason I shouldn't, he left me long ago, ditched me, told me lies, 5,000 francs, if he's offering that sort of money he wants something special, of course he does.

'I don't want your money,' she said. 'Get out of here. I've told you, I don't want to see you any more. You must have had a key made the last time. Give it to me.'

'Come on, Nicole,' he said. '6,000 francs. Take it. I'd like to stay a few days and I'll need the key to get in and out.'

'You're not staying,' she said. 'I told you before. Give me the key.'

'Sorry. No.'

'I'll change the lock.'

'You won't. You're my wife. I have a right to be here.'

'You have no right. We've been through all that.'

He sat down at the kitchen table as if he owned it. 'It's only for a few days,' he said. 'I have to get in touch with someone to find out my next move. In the meantime, nobody in the whole world knows I'm here. It's the perfect place for me, just now.'

'There isn't any perfect place for you any more,' she said. 'Your picture was in *Le Provençal* last month.'

'That? It's a police photo, years old. Even you wouldn't know me from it.'

He folded the 500-franc notes into a roll, put a rubber band around it and tossed it on the table. 'There you are, dear,' he said. 'Now, why not go out and buy us a nice dinner. And get some more meat for our dog. Eh, Bobi? Come here, boy.'

Poor Bobi, blind, hearing his name, got up and came tail-wagging towards the sound. He reached down and fondled the dog's ears. 'What about a steak, Bobi? Let's buy him a nice horse steak. Why not? Nothing's too good for our dog.'

The liar. *Our dog*. 'Bobi?' she said. 'Come here.'

Bobi ducked his head from under those false fondling fingers and came up to her, putting his nose in her skirt. She turned and went out of the kitchen,

Bobi behind her. She went into her bedroom, shut the door, locked it, then lay down. Bobi clambered on to the foot of the bed and settled in at her feet. Poor Bobi, lying there, his muzzle between his paws. He'll fall asleep now. When he sleeps, what does he dream? Does he remember the days when he was a little puppy? When Pierre first brought him to me in Hyères, sixteen years ago, you could pick him up with one hand. Does he remember those days? Does he remember the flat in Hyères? I'll never forget the first time I saw him. Pierre came into the room and said, 'I have something for you.' And I said, 'Whatever it is, I don't want it.'

'Wait,' he said. 'It's in the car.'

I remember I went to the kitchen window and looked out. I thought: So he's bought a car now that he's left me. Him that wouldn't go out in the daytime for fear someone would recognize him, now he's driving around in a car. And sure enough, I saw a 2CV parked in the yard. I saw him reach into the car to get the present, whatever it was. I thought it would be flowers or chocolates and I was ready to throw his present back at him, but he came across the yard and up the stairs with this lovely little puppy in his arms. The bastard! Back in those days I'd said over and over again that I wanted a dog and, over and over again, he'd said no, we might have to move in a hurry, maybe the next place they wouldn't allow us to keep a dog.

'Where did you get it?' I asked. Knowing him he could have stolen it.

He handed the puppy over to me. I remember thinking it had the most lovely, loving eyes. I could have kissed it.

'It's an Alsatian,' he said. 'I had six of those when I

104

was in the *milice*. They're police dogs. We can train him.'

'Train him? What's happened, the police haven't stopped looking for you, have they?'

He shook his head. 'I mean, when I come to visit.'

'You're not coming to visit, do you hear? I'm finished with you.'

'What will you call him?' he said. 'He's a boy dog. What about Putzi? One of the dogs I had in the *milice* was Putzi, he was a great dog, championship bloodlines, he'd belonged to Commander Knab himself, remember I told you about Knab. He's the one who said I was a perfect Nordic type.'

'You're a perfect shit, that's what you are. You and your Putzi! Anyway, I'm not taking him.'

She put the puppy down on the floor.

'OK, I'll let him off in some alley,' he said. 'I don't want him. I bought him for you. You wouldn't let him starve, would you?'

'He's not mine.'

'He is, now. Listen, Nicole, I just couldn't stay away any longer. I know it's risky for me to come back but I've missed you. It's been awful. I dream about you every night. Come on. Let me stay for a while.'

'No.'

'Just for a week, all right?'

'I know why you came back. And after you've fucked me a few times, you'll be off again. Where did you get that car? Did you steal it?'

'Friends of mine lent it to me,' he said. 'Priests. I'm staying with them. They're helping me. I'm learning to type. They're going to find permanent work for me, typing up student theses for the Collège St Christophe in Aix. It's not much but it will help.'

105

'Help who?'

'I'll send you some as soon as I make some.'

'I wasn't asking for money,' she said. 'I'm finished with you. I don't need you. I've got a new job.'

'Aren't you still working for the nuns?'

'I left that. I'm working as a chambermaid at the Hôtel Majestic. Believe it or not, it pays better than the nuns.'

'A chambermaid? My wife is a chambermaid. A chambermaid. My God, what next?'

'I'm not your wife. You saw the name on the door. Maranne. It's my name, not that false one you use. Pou-Pou-Pou—Pouliot!'

'You call yourself Madame, don't you?'

'I have to. But I'm not Madame. I'm nothing.'

'You're my wife in the eyes of God. We were married in the church. That's the only marriage that counts.'

'Tell that to the *mairie*. You're wanted by the police. You'll never get a marriage certificate.'

'All right, all right. Abbé Feren is working on that.'

'Is he? Do you think I'm stupid? I happen to know that if Abbé Feren walked into the *mairie* today and told them he'd married us without a licence he'd go to jail for it.'

'Who told you that?'

It was Jacquot, but I didn't tell him. The puppy came across the kitchen floor, tail frisking, and rubbed its little head against my ankle. The puppy. Bobi. That was his clever trick. He knew I'd keep that lovely little puppy. I had to. He'd said he'd dump it in some alley. He would. And I was right, he'd come back for sex, only sex. I was young then and I was pretty. Two hours later he was pulling down my pants and showing me a hard-on like a steel bar. A

106

week later he was gone. Sex was the big thing with him in those days, although he pretended to be fucking me because it was our duty before God to have a child. Oh yes, he wanted a child, but not for any normal reason. A child would be a way of holding on to me and proving to his friends, the priests, that he was a good family man, persecuted by the Jews, et cetera.

'You're not religious,' I told him once. 'It's all an act with you.'

'Is it? God forgive you for saying that. You don't know me, you have no idea how much my faith means to me. You don't know how hard it is for me that I can't go to mass like anybody else, for fear somebody will recognize me.'

'What are you talking about? You don't go to mass now because you can't stand seeing black people kneeling beside you in church, you can't stand it when the priest faces you and prays in French instead of turning his back and mumbling in Latin the way it was when you were an altar boy.'

'Well, that's true enough,' he said. 'These left-wing priests have ruined the beauty of the mass, they're ruining our religion. Not that you care, Nicole. You'll never understand what these things mean to me. You've never had an ounce of faith.'

'That's not true,' I said. 'You're a liar. You're the biggest liar I know. All that talk about how you've become another person since you met Monsignor Le Moyne, I'll tell you what that is, it's shit. Monsignor Le Moyne is just the latest dupe for your line of bullshit. "Father, forgive me, hear my confession. Only you can save me. Only you can bring me back to God." You know as well as I do that you're a con man with priests. Remember Abbé Feren?'

107

And it's true. The very first time I met him he was with this priest, Abbé Feren, an old fool who was a chaplain to the *milice*. Talk about drama! Bursting in on me that night in my place in Marseille as I was eating supper, this old priest holding him by the one arm and Jacquot holding him by the other, and him bleeding away, the blood dripping down on the floor, this tall blond guy, I thought he was some German deserter. He didn't look French. They put him down on my couch, he looked as if he was going to pass out, and Jacquot said, 'Nicole, this is Pierre Brossard, he was my chief in the *milice*, so the FFI are after him. One of them recognized him on the Canebière just now and took a shot at him. This is Abbé Feren. We went to him first and he's going to help us but we can't stay at his place.'

'Good evening, Mademoiselle,' says this old priest. 'You're Jacquot's sister, aren't you?'

'I am, Father.'

'The Abbé knows a doctor who'll come here and take the bullet out,' Jacquot said. 'Nicole, we need your help. Pierre could sleep on your couch.'

It was Jacquot who'd got me that apartment in the first place, he got it for me in 1943, when the Rosenthal family was shipped off to Germany and the *milice* requisitioned their place: 171 Rue Paradis, Marseille, that was the address, it was the only nice apartment I've ever had and Jacquot, God rest his soul, always said, 'I'm your big brother and there's only the two of us and my job is to look after you.' And he did. So if he asked me a favour there was no refusing him. I had to take this fellow in.

The doctor came later that night and took the bullet out and then Abbé Feren and Jacquot left me alone with Pierre and when I'd made up the living-room couch as a bed, and given him some soup, he thanked me, he wept, he could always turn the tears on, and later, when I looked in to see if he was all right, he'd got out of bed and was kneeling beside it, saying his prayers. And I knew what the *miliciens* were like and this wasn't like any *milicien* I'd ever known. Including Jacquot. Making the sign of the cross. Saying prayers. And he was good-looking in that blond Nazi way. The truth was, I fell for his looks, I fell for his whole act. I nursed him for three weeks and he was smart, he didn't try to fuck his friend's little sister, he was all respect and gratitude and then he told me he'd fallen in love with me and in those days just after the war when everything had gone wrong and my own brother was sentenced to death *in absentia* and I was working like a nigger in the Fabrice Mounier, I wanted a man, I wanted a child, I wanted to be happy, to be ordinary, to be like everybody else.

Fat chance. How could I be like everybody else when I was mixed up with Pierre. Did he ever love me? If you asked me to tell you what Pierre's like in one word I'd say 'liar'. Everything was lies. Even the story about the FFI shooting him was a lie. I was on the toilet one day, a couple of years after that, we were living in Hyères then, and Jacquot had come to see him and they didn't know I was at home. And I heard Jacquot say, 'I don't know. I'm fed up. We still have the guns. We could have another go at it.'

'It's too risky,' Pierre said. 'Look what happened last time.'

'That was your fault,' Jacquot said. 'You panicked.'

'I never panicked. And I told you. It's not like when we were in Paris. Marseille is different. It's

109

lousy with *flics*.'

'It wasn't lousy with *flics*, that day,' Jacquot said. 'There was only one *flic* and it was an accident that he saw us. If you hadn't run, he wouldn't have fired.'

'How do you know?' Pierre said. 'Look, what we're doing now is easy. Sure, it's boring, day after day sitting with an iron in your hand. But it's a lot less risky than what we did in Paris. I'm not going back to that.'

'So you're not interested?' Jacquot said.

'No.'

I didn't ask Pierre. He'd lie. I asked Jacquot. 'I heard you this afternoon. You told me it was the FFI who tried to shoot Pierre that time. Were the pair of you lying to me?'

'Just trying to protect you.'

'And what's this about an iron? What's that mean? I thought you and Pierre were doing factory work at Renault.'

Jacquot laughed. 'Is that what he told you? How could we? We've no papers.'

'So what *is* this?'

'It's a job. They're fake banknotes. They look too new. Our job is to iron them and fold them until they can pass for real.'

'And how long have you been doing this?'

'Ever since we came to Hyères. Look, what else can we do? The Yids and the commies are out for our hides. The courts are full of commie judges. The *flics* will·get a medal if they bring us in. That's why Pierre moved here. There isn't any legal job we can do. Do you know how boring it is to sit there day after day ironing banknotes that you can't even spend because if you stole one of those false notes the guys we work for would break our legs. Anyway, I'm fed up. I'm

110

going back to Paris.'

Poor Jacquot. He did. And two years later. Cancer.

*   *   *

She heard him call from the kitchen.
'Nicole?'
She didn't answer.
He knocked on the bedroom door.
'Nicole, are you there?'
Bobi covered his head with his paws and began to whimper. She got up, went to Bobi and comforted him. 'Stop that knocking,' she said. 'You're frightening Bobi.'
'I'll do more than frighten him,' he said. 'Unless you open up.'
And he would too. She unlocked the door.
'Listen to me,' he said. 'It's only for a few days. I'll be out of here by Monday. In the meantime, if you want peace and quiet, just do as I say. I don't want to leave this flat. I want my meals cooked here and cooked properly. Buy some good wine. Do as you're told. And if you do, I promise you Bobi will be a happy doggy. Won't you, Bobi?'
He went over to Bobi and put his hand out to pat him. But Bobi knew. Bobi couldn't see him but he knew. That dog was uncanny. He snapped at that hand, Bobi who wouldn't hurt a fly, who never in sixteen years had snapped at anybody.
'Leave Bobi alone,' she said. 'Do you hear me, leave him alone!'
'It's up to you whether I leave him alone or not.'
No human being was capable of the love Bobi had for her. And she knew it.

111

'All right,' she said. 'Come on, Bobi. Let's go shopping.'

CHAPTER FOURTEEN

From the very first time he saw Nicole he had lusted after her. He remembered lying on the couch in the living room of her little flat on Rue Paradis, seeing her pass by, half-naked, going to the shower or into her room, unable to touch her because of Jacquot. She was just a kid, jailbait, and living with her like that, he thought about it all the time. It was not being able to touch her that made him so hot for her, but it was also a time when he was changing, when God had come back into his life. In the forties he had drifted away from his boyhood faith, from mass and confession and the memory of kneeling down nightly with his parents to say the family rosary. He had lived a rough life in the years he fought for the Maréchal and for France. There were no saints in the *milice*. But then, in those first post-war years, the years of the hold-ups, the black market, the counterfeit notes, he had met Abbé Feren and begun to think again about heaven and hell. In those days, living in Nicole's little flat, he had begun to pray again. Nightly. He had been condemned to death *in absentia*. The thought of death, of capture, led him back to God. And to this Abbé who understood what it was like to have been in the *milice*, and be abandoned when the communists won the war. 'My son, of course you have committed sins in the past,' Abbé Feren said. 'But God's mercy is infinite. He forgives our sins and asks only that we sin no more.' He wanted to believe

112

the Abbé. In those years everyone wanted to be forgiven. The clergy, the politicians in the National Assembly, people in shops and factories and on the farms, every sensible person said that what happened in the war years was best forgotten, that the war trials were revenge, not justice, that the Resistance had been run by the communists and now they planned to hand the country over to Stalin. And, of course, who did the communists hate more than an ex-*milicien*? He was a victim of the times, wasn't that the truth? He wanted to get married, to hide away from the past, to live a quiet life. Abbé Feren knew about the temptations of the flesh. He knew that it wasn't possible to get a marriage certificate. But the Abbé was a saint. He told him he would marry him in the only way that counts, in church in the sight of God. And after Abbé Feren had married him to Nicole in the sight of God, there was a time, and he remembered it well, when he would lie in bed on a Sunday morning, waiting for her to come back from mass, and when she would come into the bedroom in her Sunday best, her missal in her hand, he would make her take off all her clothes and lie there on the bed, and he'd lie there beside her with his cock sticking up, looking at her naked body, telling himself that he could have her any way he wanted and all the time and be without sin in doing it. Never before had he fucked a girl without knowing he'd have to tell it in confession. But now that he had returned to God, now that he tried to live in a state of grace, now that Abbé Feren had heard his confession and given him absolution, it was a good thing he was no longer tempted by that sin. The Abbé, and later Monsignor Le Moyne, always thought of him as a devout Catholic who obeyed the commandments.

113

And he was. He had a young wife with a lovely milk-white arse and there was no sin in doing it.

Of course, later, he fell from the true path. In the sixties, when he had to leave Hyères and start a life of living in monasteries and presbyteries, no matter how much he prayed, there was always temptation, loose girls on street corners, showing their thighs. He was only human. He had money. Money from the priests, money from his typing, and, later on, the Commissaire's payments. So he could afford it. But each time he did it, each time he fell from grace, he did not go to Monsignor Le Moyne, his confessor, but anonymously, to some *curé* who didn't know him. Those were special confessions in which he confessed just that one sin.

*   *   *

'Come on, Bobi. This way.'

He heard the front door shut. Blind old beast, it should have been put down years ago. And Nicole. Poor bitch, what use is she to anyone now? Old and ugly, no kids, no relatives, except for me, if you can call me a relative, her brother's dead long ago, what kind of life is it for her, living in this little shithole of an apartment, taking the bus to La Napoule six days a week to clean up other people's dirt. She's not even religious. Her religion is that dog. 6,000 francs I gave her. How long would it take her to earn that much? She'll spend it on the dog. Well, that's all right. It's Yid money. Give it to the dog. It's all part of what's happening now, I know it, the roulette wheel's turned against me. It's bad-luck time.

He got up, went to the kitchen dresser and opened the bottom drawer. A half-used litre of *gros rouge* and a bottle of cheap *porto*. He took a glass and tried the *porto*. Too sweet, but better than nothing. I told her to buy good wine. She'll do as she's told. Remember, no one in the whole world knows I'm here, not even the Commissaire. I told him Aix. It's risky, though. He might phone there to check up on me. I'll ring him Sunday. I'll say I'm still in Aix.

He finished the *porto* then went into her bedroom and lay down on her bed. He felt his pulse. Eighty-six. Calm down. I need a rest. I need a good night's sleep. This bed's big enough for both of us. I'll eat a big dinner, drink some wine, go to sleep. Not to dream. No dreams.

But he dreamed.

*   *   *

Legrand was excited. 'Execution squad! Execution squad! Lecussan told Knab we'll shoot fifteen. OK? Who will I take?'

'Come with me.' He got up from his desk, from the papers, the damn papers that took up so much of his time. This was more like it. As chief of the second section it's my pick, my authority. Now I'll see the fear in their eyes.

In the big room there were forty-six of them, most of them Resistance, plus some Jews rounded up in the past month. Which was which? He went in with Legrand behind him. He stood very straight, his beret at a proper angle, his trousers, shirt, boots, immaculate. Prisoners who were walking around in the big room stopped at the sight of him. The others lying on the stinking straw on which they slept rolled over and got to their feet, afraid that they'd be kicked if they did not. He shouted an order. At once, six miliciens *came*

115

running upstairs and into the big room. They pointed sub-machine guns at the prisoners. The prisoners stood, stock still. They did not look at the men with guns. They looked at him. It was the moment of joy, the moment of power. I am God. I am God!

Legrand looked to him. 'At your orders, my Commandant.'

He stood silent for almost a minute. Then he said, 'Drop your trousers. All of you.'

They started unbuttoning. Trousers fell around their ankles. He gestured. 'Pull down your pants. Get your pricks out.'

Forty-six men turned in his direction, all of them with their pricks hanging out. He took his revolver from its holster, and went to the first man. With the barrel of the revolver, he jerked the penis up for a better look, then the next, the next, the next. The fourth man had a black-looking prick, circumcised. 'Jew?' he asked.

The man hung his head and was silent. 'Yes, he's a Yid,' Legrand said.

He nodded to the miliciens. *They herded the man into a corner. He felt, now, the rush of power, the moment of life and death. Keep them in suspense. The Resistants don't know what I'm after. He walked to the next group of men and again, flicked their penises with his revolver barrel. Again, the fourth man was a Yid. He gestured. Legrand began to grin. The other boys too. They knew the game now. But he did not smile. He felt the rush of power go right to his own prick. He had a hard-on. He picked only Yids, only those whose foreskins had been cut off long ago by some stinking rabbi.*

But there were only fourteen Yids in that batch of forty-six. Never mind. He lined them up in a row. 'Pull

116

up your trousers,' he told the room. 'That's all, for now.'

But then Legrand asked the question and he answered it. He said the thing about the Yids, the thing that fucked everything, the thing that made this dream come back, again, again, the bad-luck dream, the thing the Yids quoted in the complaint against him, the thing that made it a crime against humanity.

'There's only fourteen here, chief. Lecussan's asked for fifteen.'

'We're short one Yid,' he said. 'I want Yids, only Yids. That's all. Dismiss.'

Fourteen Yids. He had driven out with Legrand in the car he'd requisitioned from Lehmann before he sent Lehmann to Auschwitz in that last big draft of Jews, ordered by Monsieur Le Préfet. It was a yellow Panhard roadster, the top down, very smart. The execution squad and their prisoners followed in a farm truck. When they arrived at the cemetery, he ordered the Jews to be lined up against the cemetery wall. 'Are the cards ready?' he asked Drumont. He had ordered fourteen pieces of cardboard with the Jews' names on them.

'Why the cards, chief?' Legrand asked.

'To impress the population.'

The boys in the firing squad laughed at that. They were nervous. Firing squads were always nervous.

He liked executions. They were a form of war. The enemy was cornered and in his power. He was God. He gave the order.

Sub-machine guns. They fired in bursts, but even with sub-machine guns, you had to make sure. There must be no witness. He and Legrand walked down the line, giving the coup de grâce, a bullet in the back of the neck. That stopped their moaning. And their twitching.

117

'Feet against the wall,' he ordered.

The squad lined the dead men up in a row, their feet touching the wall. 'Tie on the name tags,' he ordered. The tags were tied around the men's necks. One of the corpses gave some sort of final convulsion and the name card twisted under him, hidden from view.

'It doesn't matter,' he said. 'Let's go.'

*   *   *

'Will you stop it?' Nicole said. 'Twitching like that, you'll pitch me out of the bed.'

He came up from the dream. 'I wasn't twitching,' he said. 'It was a dead Yid.'

CHAPTER FIFTEEN

'But why me?' Valentin asked Professor Proulx, who was climbing the great stone staircase of the archbishopric, one step ahead of him. Professor Proulx, who was old and stout, did not answer, preserving his breath until they reached the top. He then paused and said, 'Gorchakov. He's on the list of your interviewees, isn't he?'

'Yes, but I haven't talked to him, as yet.'

'Well, the Cardinal told me it's to do with Gorchakov. So I thought you should be present.'

Professor Proulx was the chairman of the Cardinal's commission and the author of a definitive book on the history of modern France. Valentin was somewhat in awe of him. He wondered who else would attend this special meeting. He remembered reading the dossier: Dom Vladimir Gorchakov,

118

Carmelite monk, Abbot of the Abbaye de St Cros, a graduate of *Normale Sup*, an aide to Maréchal Pétain in the first years of Vichy before leaving to join the Carmelite Order, a White Russian aristocrat, his mother a Georgian princess, murdered by the Soviets, a religious conservative, hostile to the Cardinal's liberal views. The very portrait of a cleric who might shelter Brossard.

The Cardinal stood, his back to a large window that gave on to the Place de la Fourvière. On his right was a priest, who had been introduced as Father Thiers of the Society of Jesus. On the Cardinal's left, at ease on a sofa, was Monsignor Flandin, Secretary of the Episcopal Committee on Relations with Judaism. The Cardinal, tall, stooped, bowed his head slightly in welcome and asked Proulx and Valentin to be seated. He himself remained standing, absent-mindedly pulling on his long nose with his forefinger and thumb.

'Gentlemen, this is something that directly concerns you as members of our commission. But I would ask you to keep it in the strictest confidence. Remember, we are not policemen. It's not our business to deliver Brossard into the hands of the law. I say this because of something that has happened in the past few days. Dom Vladimir Gorchakov, of the Abbey of St Cros, near Salon, telephoned me on Monday night to tell me that Brossard has been staying for the past month as his guest in the monastery and that he left, abruptly, some days ago. On the day after Brossard left the police arrived at the monastery and told the Abbot that a foreign tourist had been murdered and his car dumped in a ravine a few miles from St Cros. The police asked if Dom Vladimir or one of the other monks was expecting a

119

visitor. They were not. There were no papers on the dead man and his wallet was missing, but he was identified as a Canadian through a record of the driver's licence he presented when he rented the car from a company in Marseille. The name on the licence registration was, Dom Vladimir noticed, a Jewish one. As we know, at least two Jewish groups are trying to find Brossard and bring him to justice. Later the police returned to tell Dom Vladimir that the dead man's Canadian driver's licence had proved to be false. Dom Vladimir did not, of course, tell the police anything about Brossard and his abrupt departure on the day of the murder. But he called Dom André Vergnes, principal of a Cistercian school in Aix, and an old friend of his, where Brossard sometimes lodged on leaving Salon, and warned him of what had happened. Two days later he received a call from Dom André, saying that, indeed, Brossard had turned up there, asking to be taken in as a guest. Dom André, who had in the past lodged Brossard and helped him financially, believing him to be a victim of long-standing persecution, now, for the first time, became suspicious of him and sent him away. These two clerics then decided that, because of the possibility that Brossard might be linked to this murder, it was their duty to inform me that they had sheltered him. Dom Vladimir, in particular, worries that if the dead man *was* a Jew who was on the point of tracking down Brossard, Brossard might have killed him, taken his papers and wallet and tried to make it look like a robbery. I've called you here today because if, indeed, Brossard is mixed up in this terrible affair and it's discovered that the Church is still sheltering him, I will be hounded by the media for an explanation. Of course I won't deny the facts, but I think it's now extremely urgent that the commission furnish me with some answers.'

'What sort of answers?' Professor Proulx asked.

'A preliminary report would be very helpful,' the Cardinal said. 'It will show that we are honestly trying to track down the Church's involvement with Brossard. We should also, if possible, provide some tentative explanation for the help he has received from many clerics over the past years.'

Monsignor Flandin held up his hand. 'Gentlemen, there is also the tricky question of the Jewish community's reaction, if we admit that we are still sheltering Brossard. I have assured the Grand Rabbi that we are not.'

'But we *are* sheltering him,' the Jesuit said. 'And despite Your Eminence's instructions, there are clerics who will continue to shelter him. So we've got to find out who they are. I've been looking into this matter and there's obviously a pattern. Brossard seems to have certain routes that he travels each year, certain monasteries and convents that he visits regularly and which provide him with food, lodging and, sometimes, employment of sorts.'

He turned to Professor Proulx. 'The preliminary findings of the commission bear me out on that, don't they, sir?'

'They do,' Proulx said. 'But the circle of his support is now considerably narrower than in the past. Professor Valentin tells me that the new charge against him of a crime against humanity, and the national publicity it has received, has changed many priests' minds about his innocence.'

'I wouldn't count on it,' the Jesuit said, and gave a nervous giggle. 'In the Church, very often, devotion replaces intelligence.'

121

'Eminence, have you talked again to Dom Vladimir or Dom André?' Proulx asked. 'If they've changed their minds about Brossard, perhaps they may be able to help us?'

'I've talked to them both. I told them we want above all to avoid any further publicity in this matter and therefore we have no intention of finding Brossard in order to hand him over to the police. But when I asked Dom Vladimir where we might look for Brossard he said only that, in the past, Brossard told him that he sometimes went from Aix to stay with clerical friends in Nice.'

'What friends, sir?' Valentin asked.

The Cardinal gave him a cold, sidelong glance, then turned to look out of the window. The sun had begun to set on the Place de la Fourvière. 'Professor, I repeat, I haven't asked you and Professor Proulx to come here this morning to act as detectives. It's our job, I mean Father Thiers' and mine, to find out who these people are and to put a stop to it. When we do, I will, of course, give you all the information in our possession.'

Professor Proulx said politely, 'Eminence, I'm sure Professor Valentin wasn't trying to pry.'

'Of course not,' the Cardinal said, turning back from the window with a thin, polite smile. 'We all have much work to do. Poor Monsignor Flandin here will have, perhaps, the most difficult task of all, if he is forced to explain this almost unexplainable situation to the Jewish community. In the meantime, gentlemen, I would be very grateful if you would consult with the other members of the commission to see if it is possible for you to issue some sort of a preliminary report, something that will indicate that we are, indeed, involved in a thorough investigation of these events. But remember, if you tell the others about this latest development, you must warn them to keep it in strictest confidence. As you can see I'm in a very difficult position, at present.'

Proulx stood up and glanced at Valentin indicating that they should leave. 'Eminence, I'll be frank. Our task, as outlined by you, is to prepare a full and comprehensive report on these events. It must be impartial and it must not be hurried. So, for the moment, I can't assure you that my fellow historians and I will agree to issue a preliminary report before we have all the facts. But I will be guided by our consensus on this matter.'

'That's all I ask,' the Cardinal said. 'And thank you very much for coming. You'll let me know, of course?'

'Yes, Your Eminence. We will.'

*   *   *

Minutes later, as they descended the great stone staircase, Proulx said, 'I told him the truth, didn't I?'

'What do you mean, sir?'

'A preliminary report is just damage-control. That's what he wants. We'd simply be seen as Church apologists if we do as he suggests. Those weren't the terms of our instruction.'

'Not only that,' Valentin said. 'But that colonel of gendarmerie I spoke to should be told about this. By keeping it from him, we're assisting in the obstruction of justice.'

'I wouldn't go that far, Professor. It's not our place to inform the police. That's a matter for the Cardinal's conscience. I think we must leave that decision up to him.'

123

Must we? Valentin thought. But he held his tongue.

CHAPTER SIXTEEN

'Who's calling, please?'

'Tell him it's Monsieur Pierre.'

When Rosa heard the name she felt her heart jump. Henri had told her, 'If he calls and I'm not here, make sure you get an address or, at least, a telephone number. Tell him I said it's urgent that we get in touch.'

'Monsieur Pierre,' she said. 'Good. The Commissaire is expecting to hear from you. Don't hang up, please. I'll see if I can find him.'

'Thank you, Madame.'

She went through the kitchen and into the garden. She wasn't sure if Henri had left yet. He'd said he might drive over to the vineyard before lunch. 'Henri?' she called. 'Henri?'

'What?' An irritated voice came from the potting shed at the bottom of the garden. He came out, slapping his hands together to get rid of the dirt.

'Telephone. It's him.'

He nodded and, walking more quickly than usual, went into the house. When she followed him into the kitchen she saw his left leg begin to jiggle as he picked up the phone in the front hall. So something was wrong, very wrong.

'Vionnet here.'

'Monsieur Pierre, sir. Sir, do you have any news for me?'

'News about what? Where are you?'

'Remember, last time we talked, sir, you said you'd check on the passport I gave you. And you'd try to find out about that group.'

'Don't you read the newspapers?' the Commissaire asked angrily. 'The Salon police found the number of the driver's licence to be a fraud. So the passport is probably false.'

'I'm sorry, sir. I missed that. I've been moving around, as you know.'

'Where are you? Aix?'

'That's why I'm calling, sir. This group, whoever they are, knew where I was going to be in Aix. They had someone waiting for me outside the St Christophe priory yesterday morning. Luckily, I gave him the slip.'

'So where are you, now? Dammit, man, I must know where to find you.'

'Of course, sir. That's why I called. I spent last night in a motel outside Aix. I'm on my way to Nice, now.'

'To the address you gave me? Friends of the ex-Archbishop of Dakar?'

'Sir, that's why I'm calling. If this group has tracked me twice, in each case because I went to the usual place on my list, then perhaps they'll track me there.'

'You could be right,' the Commissaire said. 'Do you have an alternative?'

'I have a great friend, the almoner of the Carmelite abbey at Villefranche. The Abbot there is a member of the Chevaliers and knows me well. I haven't been there in the past two years. But I'm sure they will receive me.'

'You'll arrive when?'

'Tomorrow, sir. But I wanted to check with you.

Have you any news at all for me?'

'News about what?'

'About this group. You'll admit it's very worrying.'

'When I have news for you, I'll give it to you. What's the address and telephone number of the abbey?'

'The abbey is on the Haute Corniche just outside Villefranche, sir. There is no street number but it's four kilometres past a resort hotel called the Bristol. The abbey's telephone number is 93 65 32 97.'

'Good. Phone me tomorrow. Without fail, do you hear? You're sure they'll take you in?'

'Yes, sir. But if anything goes wrong, I'll let you know.'

'Do that.'

Commissaire Vionnet put down the phone. As he did, Rosa called out from the kitchen, '*Chéri*, I've made sausage with lentils for lunch. Are you ready to eat?'

'In a moment. First, I must make a phone call.'

CHAPTER SEVENTEEN

History is an echo, Valentin thought as he walked the stone paths of the Tuileries gardens beside his interlocutor. Today's echo is of de Gaulle's victory march down the Champs-Elysées forty-four years ago. To historians every year is an anniversary. To ordinary people the past is entombed. He looked through the ornate Tuileries railings at the Hôtel Meurice on the adjoining Rue de Rivoli. Who among these shoppers passing its windows knows or cares that in the years of Occupation it was the seat of the German Kommandatura in Paris?

'What year were you born, Colonel?' he asked his interlocutor.

''42.'

'So we're the same generation. I was born in the spring of '43.'

'In Lille?'

'No, in Bayeux. And you?'

'Me? Dijon,' Colonel Roux said.

'And we're both too young to remember the war.'

'I remember it only as something my parents talked about,' Roux said.

'Mine didn't.'

'Mine did,' Roux said. 'My father was a butcher. He used to tell us stories about RAF pilots being picked up and sent home through a Resistance chain. He said he was part of that chain. The Resistance. Of course, everyone claimed to be in it. Afterwards.'

'If only my parents *had* been in it,' Valentin said. 'Or told us some believable lie. But they didn't. When my sister and I asked about those days they said, "You wouldn't understand." My parents had a drapery shop in Bayeux. They kept it going all through the Occupation. And of course, like most small-business people, they saw the end of the war as a victory for the communists. When I think back, I realize they were against things, not for them. Pétain? My father simply said he was too old to lead France. After the war they voted for de Gaulle, but I don't think they bought his *folie des grandeurs*. What were they for, I wonder? What were their ideals? They certainly didn't seem to have any during the Occupation years.'

'It's hard to pass judgement on what people did

127

back then,' the colonel said. 'We haven't lived with Germans walking up and down our streets. France had lost the war. Pétain was an old war hero, perfect casting as the honest broker between France and Hitler. Who was de Gaulle? Some jumped-up general in London, someone our parents had never heard of, someone working with the British who'd let France down, someone who sounded like a potential dictator. And let's be honest, de Gaulle's primary interest wasn't fighting the Germans and winning the war. It was making sure the Anglo-Saxons accepted him as the leader of Free France and that France would emerge as one of the winning team. *And* claiming a victory France didn't deserve.'

'You're not a Gaullist, I see.'

'No. I was a socialist once. Now, I don't know.'

'I was just thinking of de Gaulle,' Valentin said. 'Hard to believe that it's forty-four years since the Liberation.'

'Yes, but what does that mean to a twenty year old?'

'I wonder. I suppose they'd consider us fools for trying to bring to justice some old French fascist who killed Jews before this generation was born.'

'I know,' Roux said. 'Yet, I consider this the most important case of my career.'

Valentin glanced sideways at him, a tall, military figure, his head up, his step brisk. Suddenly, Roux paused in his stride and said, 'Because of that I'm grateful for what you've done today. You've given me two avenues of pursuit. One is to look more closely at this murder. Do the Salon police know something they haven't released to the public? Also, your information has opened up more strongly the line I used with Monsignor Le Moyne.'

128

'Which was?'

'I put into his mind that I'm a less dangerous pursuer than these Jewish avengers. I believe it had an effect. It will, I hope, have a similar effect if I use the same tactic with our friend Dom Vladimir Gorchakov. If someone's betraying Brossard to this group, I've got to get to him before they do. For both these reasons I'm going to Salon.'

'When?'

'Tonight.'

* * *

'*Bourride!*' Inspector Cholet pronounced the word like an actor announcing a pageant. 'Colonel, today is the one day, the only day of the week, in which Mère Michèle prepares it for luncheon at her restaurant, the Tout Va Bien. When you telephoned me this morning I took the liberty of reserving a table for two. In the pantheon of fish stew, Mère Michèle's *bourride* is the summa.'

Roux, estimating the inspector's weight at closer to three than two hundred pounds, realized that this lunch would not be a matter of forty minutes. And, indeed, when they arrived at the Tout Va Bien, a workers' restaurant a few streets behind the Salon Préfecture de Police, they were shown, with the special handshakes and greetings accorded to regular patrons, to a table in a secluded alcove, ideal for a tête-à-tête. Inspector Cholet seated himself with his back to the wall, a chequered napkin tucked into his shirt collar, a glass of Chablis in his hand, with the air of a man whose afternoon at the office will be short.

But he listened carefully. He was, Roux guessed, one of those affable fat men who successfully conceal

129

the razor-sharp inquisitor lurking within their bonhomous responses. The story Roux had elected to tell him was an edited version of Valentin's discoveries, namely how, through a confidential source, Roux's office had learned that Brossard had been a guest in the Abbaye de St Cros and had left abruptly on the evening of the day of the murder. Roux emphasized that he, as the officer in charge of the hunt for Brossard, was giving this information to Inspector Cholet because he felt it his duty to inform him that there might be a connection between Brossard and the murder. In return, he asked if there were any elements in the case which the Salon police had not made public.

'You know, of course, that we have interrogated the Abbot of St Cros?' the inspector said.

'So I've been told. He did not, I imagine, mention that he had played host to a wanted criminal?'

'Indeed, he did not. Although when I looked up our records, I discovered that back in '71, just before the presidential pardon, we visited the abbey to make inquiries in this connection. The inquiries, I admit, were perfunctory. And of course, after the pardon, the inquiry was dropped.'

'But later, when the new charge came out—the complaint of a crime against humanity—wasn't the inquiry reinstated?'

The inspector smiled and, reaching across the table, refilled Roux's glass. 'Officially, yes. The inquiry, as you know, was run from the *préfecture* in Paris. All I can tell you is that, here in Salon, we were not asked to check on whether Brossard was still in this region.'

'That's odd.'

The inspector shrugged. 'Yes, I must admit, I do

130

find it odd. There are those who say the police didn't really want to find him. As I wasn't personally involved, I don't know if that's true or false. I hope it's the latter. In any event, I want to assure you that, so far, I've received no instructions from my superiors on how I should deal with you. Therefore, as a fellow police officer, I intend to give you my full co-operation.'

'Thank you.'

'Very well, then. We're colleagues. Personally I don't care who finds Brossard. My job is to put the collar on criminals. I'm no politician. I don't suppose you are, either. So let's look at this together. Who would want to shoot him? Relatives of his victims? Most of whom were Jews. Correct?'

'Correct.'

'A Jewish group, then, Colonel. Not one of the well-known Nazi-hunters like the Klarsfelds or the Wiesenthal Centre. It's not their style. But possibly relatives of victims, people with a personal score to settle.'

'Exactly.'

'Do you know of such a group, Colonel?'

'No. It's just a hunch, a supposition.'

The inspector leaned back, sniffing the air.

'Smell that? I believe it is the *bourride*. Colonel, you're in for a treat.' He offered the bottle. 'A *petit vin blanc*?'

'Yes, thank you. It's good wine. Local?'

'From the Luberon. Our wines have greatly improved in the past decade. So, to go back to your supposition, Colonel. The question I ask myself is this. If this man was a would-be assassin and if Brossard killed him in self-defence, why did he take his money and papers?'

131

'Perhaps to make it look like a simple murder and robbery? In that way no one would connect him with it.'

'Could be,' the inspector said. 'But he forgot something. Something we *haven't* made public. There was a revolver in the glove compartment of the dead man's car. It was fitted with a silencer. Not the sort of weapon a Canadian tourist would carry on a European holiday. In addition, it was doctored. No serial numbers. In addition the dead man's clothes, his trousers, shirt, jacket, were French, not American or Canadian.'

The inspector broke off, putting down his glass and holding up his hands in a gesture of welcome.

'Ah! Here it comes, the first part of our *bourride*. And Madame herself! Colonel Roux, may I introduce you to Mère Michèle, one of our national treasures.'

Mère Michèle, accompanying the waiter who carried the first portion of *bourride*, shook hands with both the inspector and the colonel, then smilingly watched the serving of the soup.

'*Bon appetit*, Messieurs.'

When Mère Michèle had moved on, Roux sampled the *bourride*. 'Delicious. We shouldn't spoil it by talking business. But I must say I was fascinated by your comment about the dead man's gun and his clothes. Possibly the Canadian driver's licence was to throw us off the scent. It's more likely he was French and a relative of some of the Dombey Jews who were all French citizens.'

The inspector shook his head, then wiped his mouth with his napkin. 'A relative? I doubt it.'

'Why?'

'I saw the corpse. It was not circumcised.'

132

'You're sure?'

The inspector nodded. 'Quite sure. We ran a check to see if he was someone with a criminal record, a professional, hired by this group. I sent his fingerprints to Paris and I got a telex from the *préfecture* saying that there is no record of them on any files, including those of the Canadian Mounted Police.'

For Roux, at that moment, the restaurant sounds, the muted noise of conversation in the larger room, the rattle of cutlery, the thud of doors as the waiters exited from the kitchen, all blended into a confused and distant roar. The *préfecture* in Paris. He stared dully at Inspector Cholet who, smiling, watched an approaching waiter.

'Ah! Here comes the second part of our *bourride*, Colonel. I believe today's fish is turbot.'

CHAPTER EIGHTEEN

Father Jérôme, the *père hospitalier*, crossed the courtyard of the Abbaye de St Cros and entered the *atelier*. Twenty monks sat at their potting wheels. Six others were at drawing tables, working on design. Brother Julius and the Abbot were in conversation at the far end of the room. The Abbot saw him enter.

'Yes, Jérôme?'

'There is an army officer in the visitors' room, Father Abbot. He wishes to speak to you. He gave me this card.'

The Abbot glanced at the card, then put it in the sleeve of his robe. He turned to Brother Julius. 'The shipment for Dijon,' he said. 'Let me know

133

when it's ready.'

'Yes, Father Abbot.'

'Take him up to my study,' the Abbot told Jérôme. 'I'm going there now.'

As he crossed the yard and climbed the winding stairs, the Abbot took out the card and looked at it again. Gendarmerie. Army police. This new judge has transferred the dossier to the army. And it's on the dossier that Brossard has stayed with us in the past.

Dom Vladimir entered his office and went over to the rough table that served as his desk. He put the ceramics order from the Galeries Lebrun in Dijon into the box with letters to be answered. As he did, he heard a knock. He went to the door and opened it, extending his hand in welcome to the visitor.

'Colonel Roux? Good morning. Please, come in. Take a seat. What may I do for you?'

He approved of this officer. Dress uniform, gloves, impeccable *tenue*. Dom Vladimir had, in a former life, served in a cavalry regiment.

'I don't know if you're aware of it, sir, but the gendarmerie has been assigned the task of finding the fugitive, Pierre Brossard. I came to see you, to ask if you can help us with our inquiries.'

'Brossard. Yes. What did you want to know?'

'I'm told he was a guest here for a period of almost a month, earlier this year?'

'Were you indeed?' Dom Vladimir's tone was cold. 'May I ask who gave you this information?'

'I'm afraid that's confidential, sir.'

'Well, as you may know, Colonel, in most monastic orders, including ours, asylum offered to a traveller who requests it is also a confidential matter. So, before I answer your question, I'd like to know if

134

you were told this story by a lay or a clerical source.'

'A lay source, sir. But a completely reliable one.'

Dom Vladimir raised his hands in a gesture of bewilderment. 'Tell me. Who is a completely reliable source in matters of this kind? What do you know about this "source's" prejudices or priorities?'

'I believe that this informant *is* disinterested, sir.'

'No informant is completely disinterested, Colonel. To clarify matters, let me tell you *my* prejudices. I am the son of White Russian aristocrats. I was a servant of the Vichy Government before I took Holy Orders and I believe that God's mercy is superior to man's justice. I suppose that last belief, or prejudice, if you will, is the most important one in this case.'

'Again, without disrespect, Father Abbot, may I ask if you believe that clerics like yourself have the right to forgive Brossard for his crimes?'

'Our pardon is granted in the name of God in the sacrament of confession. We are instructed to grant God's pardon to all sinners who honestly repent of their sins.'

'But has Brossard ever repented, Father Abbot? According to those who pleaded his case in the past he has pretended that the killings and the tortures he committed were military actions, that everything he did, he did as a servant of Vichy, loyal to Maréchal Pétain.'

'I am not his confessor, Colonel, so I can't answer that. But Monsignor Le Moyne, who *was* his confessor, assures me that Brossard asked God's pardon for his acts and received absolution in confession. The Christian act of pardon does not countenance revenge, no matter how heinous the crimes of the sinner.'

135

'But surely, sir, that's a falsification of the Church's teachings?'

The Abbot exploded in an angry laugh. 'Indeed? Please, enlighten me on my error, Colonel.'

'It seems to me, sir, that a pardon is false which ignores those who have been injured and maltreated and which is given solely in response to a confessional oath of repentance. I think that's confusing Divine pardon with pardon given by one man to another. In this case, a pardon granted Brossard by Monsignor Le Moyne.'

'I'm afraid you've missed my point, Colonel. Be that as it may, you must remember that an official pardon *was* given by one man to another, in this case the President of the Republic who granted Brossard a pardon in '71? Yes, '71. The President believed then, as our current President believes now, that so many years after these events it's time for reconciliation, a time to put the wrongs and rancours of the years of Occupation behind us. I must say I agree with that sentiment.'

'Father Abbot, as you know, Brossard is now charged with a crime which no president has the authority to pardon, the international charge of a crime against humanity. The law must take its course. But I didn't come here this morning to ask you to do something your conscience will not permit you to do. I am asking for your help because Brossard is now in great danger. He is an old man. If he is arrested and tried before a court of law he may be acquitted, or he may spend the rest of his life in prison. In either case he will almost certainly live out his allotted span of years. But if we don't find him and take him into custody within the next few days, he may be murdered.'

136

'How do you know this?'

'You remember the tourist who was shot and his car thrown into a ravine some days ago. The police came to see you about it?'

'Yes, indeed.'

'We now believe that the dead man was a professional assassin. We believe he was hired by a Jewish commando, probably to avenge those Jews Brossard executed at Dombey. We also suspect that this group is in contact with someone who knows Brossard's pattern of movement. For he does have a pattern. We know that in the past year he has moved from one clerical residence to another, rarely staying more than a few weeks in any particular place. We also know that Cardinal Delavigne has made a request to the French clergy that, henceforth, all clerical doors be closed to him. So he must now seek out those who will ignore the Cardinal's wishes, possibly among those right-wing clerics known as "*intégristes*".'

'I am not one of them,' the Abbot said. 'They have been disavowed by Rome. However, I didn't comply with the Cardinal's request, which, by the way, is my right as Abbot of a monastic order.'

'But would you know where I might contact these "*intégristes*"? Or where I might reach Brossard?'

The Abbot rose from his desk and went to the window of his study. A misty morning sun floated over the rock-strewn ravine surrounding the monastery walls. The Abbot spoke quietly, his back to his visitor.

'You are not being honest with me, Colonel. This would be assassin was murdered, wasn't he? And you believe the man who shot him was Pierre Brossard. If I could help you find Brossard, you will put him on trial for this killing.'

'That would be a decision for the Salon police,' Roux said. 'And it wouldn't be easy for them to prove their case. Apart from the plea of self-defence, I imagine an old *milicien* like Brossard wouldn't leave any incriminating evidence. In fact, the Salon police suspect that he removed the dead man's papers for that reason.'

The Abbot turned suddenly from his contemplation of the ravine. 'So the police *do* believe that Brossard was the killer?'

'Yes, sir.'

'And you, Colonel, what do you think?'

'I believe he killed him, yes. And I also believe that this group will almost certainly send a second assassin to kill Brossard. They are obviously well organized and well informed. That's why I'm asking for your help, sir. We must find Brossard before they do.'

'Or before he kills again,' the Abbot said.

There was a moment of silence. Then, the Abbot walked back to his worktable, his heavy boots loud on the wooden boards of the study. He sat down in his chair, opened a worn leather notebook and looked up at Roux.

'Colonel, I am going to help you as much as I can. Not because I want to save Brossard from an assassin's bullet, although I do not want to see him killed. But if what you say is true, I have foolishly given shelter to a murderer, a murderer who, if threatened, may kill again. I now see that I was in error in ignoring the Cardinal's request.'

The Abbot paused and looked down at his notebook.

'So. I know something of Brossard's habits. In

138

recent years he has been supported financially by a group known as the Chevaliers de Ste Marie. Have you heard of them?'

'A Catholic lay group, isn't it?'

'Yes, about four hundred members, predominantly ultraconservative, but also including people who were members of the Resistance. As you may know, Colonel, many French Resistance fighters were as anti-communist as they were anti-Nazi. Some of them are now Chevaliers. It's a sort of crusade, anti-communist, anti-freemason. Anti the enemies of France.'

'And anti-Jewish?'

'Not openly, no. Bishop Grasset is the head of the movement and, of course, he's part of the established Church. The Chevaliers have links to the *"intégristes"*, those right-wing Catholics who have defied Rome, but the Chevaliers themselves have managed to remain within the body of the Catholic Church. As a proof of this, with the blessing of the official hierarchy, they hold an annual religious ceremony on Good Friday in Sacré Coeur basilica in Paris, where they parade in velvet capes, embroidered with a golden cross. The age of chivalry, knightly crusade, that sort of thing.'

'And you say they've been supporting Brossard financially?'

'Yes. On each occasion that he stayed with us for a period of over a month, a letter would arrive for him, containing a money order for 3,000 francs. Brossard would ask our almoner to cash it for him. The sender was not identified, but once, when we had some difficulty in cashing the order, our almoner made enquiries and found that the address it was sent from was that of the Chevaliers in Paris. When Brossard stayed with my friend Dom André Vergnes in Aix, a similar letter would arrive for him. Dom André, who knows someone highly placed in the Chevaliers, mentioned Brossard and the envelope. This friend said, "Of course. Pierre is one of us."'

'So he's a Chevalier?'

'I believe so, yes. And in that case, it's almost certain that from now on he will be helped by certain clerics who are in close touch with the Chevaliers. If he follows his usual pattern there is a certain priory in Villefranche where you might find him at present. I remember that he has stayed there, on occasion, before going on to the *"intégriste"* priory in Nice. The Villefranche prior is a religious conservative.'

'Do you have the address of this priory?'

'Yes. I'll give it to you. But there is one other fact which might be worth looking into, although I am not sure what it signifies. When Brossard was our guest here, it was his custom to go into Salon most afternoons and while away his time at a café called the Bar Montana. He would often ask our *père hospitalier* if he might use our telephone to phone this bar. And Father Jérôme, who was present at those telephone calls, remembers that it was always the same question. He would ask if his letter had arrived. Sometimes, he would become agitated if the answer was no. Make of it what you will. I just thought I'd mention it.'

'I'm glad you did, sir. And the address of the Villefranche priory?'

The Abbot unscrewed the top of his old-fashioned fountain pen and began to write.

CHAPTER NINETEEN

'A *petit vin blanc*, Inspector? And the same for your friend?' Madame Marchand signalled to her son, Jules, who was serving behind the bar. 'Roger is in the cellar. I'll get him for you.'

As Jules put the glasses before them, Inspector Cholet showed him the photographs. Jules, who was in his early twenties, picked up the second photograph, the one showing the older Brossard, and laughed. Jules wore a long ponytail and, in his right ear, a small gold earring. 'Yes, I think that's him. Old turd. Papa knows him. He had a row with him once.'

Roger Marchand, the owner of the Bar Montana, came up the staircase leading from the cellar to the trapdoor behind the bar. He shook hands with Cholet and was introduced to Roux. He looked at the second photograph and whistled. 'You mean this is Brossard, the one who was pardoned? The one *Le Meridional* writes about?'

'That's him,' Roux said. 'Of course it was taken a few years ago. He might look different today.'

'No, he's not. Shit, if I'd known who he was I'd have given him a kick in the arse a long time ago.'

'Papa, you remember the row about the *noirs*?' Jules said.

'Of course I do. It makes sense now, doesn't it? Last year when he was here he came to me in a rage because some black kids came and sat at the table next to his. We don't often get them in here, they have other cafés to go to. He started on about how could I expect customers to eat and drink off the same cups and plates that had been used by stinking *noirs*. I told

141

him, "Look, you're not a regular, you come here now and then and we're good enough to hold your post for you. If you don't like *noirs*, tell them to send your letter somewhere else."'

'But he didn't, did he?' Inspector Cholet said.

'No. He backed down when I said that.'

'This letter,' Roux said. 'Do you remember anything about it?'

'Yes, it was registered, I always had to sign for it. It came from Paris, that's all I know.'

'How often did it come?'

'Once, each time he visited here. Usually he'd be here for a few weeks and it would come a few days before he left.'

'And did he ever talk to you? Did he meet anyone here? Do you know anything else that might help?'

'No, he never spoke to anyone. He'd come in the afternoon and the thing I remember about him is he always read through *Le Monde* and that other Paris paper, *Libération*. He'd order a coffee or a beer and sit on his arse for a couple of hours. I thought he was a pensioner, maybe coming here once a year for a few weeks to visit relatives. To tell you the truth, I didn't pay him much heed.'

'He didn't like this,' Jules said, fingering his gold earring. 'Or my hairstyle.'

'And you knew him as what?' Roux asked. 'I mean, what name was on the letter that came for him?'

'Pouliot. Monsieur Pouliot. Care of Bar Montana.'

CHAPTER TWENTY

Judge Livi came through her outer office and saw the colonel waiting in her study. She stopped at her secretary's desk. 'I don't want to be disturbed. No phone calls.'

'Very good, Madame.'

She closed the study door behind her as she went in. They shook hands. 'When did you get back?'

'Late last night.'

'Success?'

'Yes. But we're on a tightrope. Or, I should say, I am. You, Madame, are my superior in this matter. Only you.'

'I don't understand.'

'I need a search warrant for a religious house and I need it at once. It will have to be prepared in the greatest secrecy. I have no idea if there could be a leak within the gendarmerie itself. But I now know that anything is possible in this case. We can't trust the police, we can't trust the ministry, we can't trust the DST. In fact, if we are to trap Brossard, we can't risk revealing our plan to any official of the French state. I'm beginning to realize that we are in a labyrinth.'

'What happened in Salon?'

'The man who was murdered was not Jewish. He was almost certainly a hired assassin. Yet when Inspector Cholet of the Salon police sent the corpse's fingerprints to Paris he received a telex telling him that there is no record of those prints on any police files. Yet if he was a professional, it's almost certain his prints would be on file somewhere. It makes me wonder. What if those prints were on file in Paris and have been removed?'

'But why?'

'I don't know. As I said, it's a labyrinth. I discovered some other things that don't fit. First, Brossard is being aided financially by a right-wing Catholic group called the Chevaliers de Ste Marie. For a long time now, they have been sending him a monthly stipend of 3,000 francs. That's understandable. But it seems he has also been receiving, regularly, a much larger sum of money from some other Paris source. Why?'

'You mentioned a labyrinth,' Judge Livi said. 'I've been in that labyrinth in the past few days, stumbling through years of dossiers. And I've come up with a few odd facts. In 1961 when right-wing Algerian *pied-noir* groups were setting off bombs in Paris to protest the Algerian war, even though Brossard was a hunted felon, the head of the government's anti-terrorist unit managed to get in touch with him, secretly, through a lawyer, asking him to act as an informer on those groups because he was known to be in touch with them. You'll remember he had acted as a police informer in the past, in the period just after 1945.'

'In the Rue des Saussaies, where he betrayed his friend Abbé Feren and others.'

'And, conveniently, was allowed to walk out of prison during the Commissaire's lunch hour,' Judge Livi said. 'An interesting point. The Commissaire from whose office he walked out free is now retired. His name is Henri Vionnet. He is mentioned in the dossiers again at the time of the Algerian attempt.'

'But Vionnet isn't anti-terrorist squad, is he?'

'No, he was regular police. He was consulted by the DST, as an expert on Brossard. He lives in

144

Avignon.' Judge Livi leaned back in her chair, put her hands together as though to pray and smiled tentatively at Roux. 'Colonel, doesn't it look as though this commissaire has known all along where to find Brossard. And what does that suggest to you?'

'That Brossard's being protected, not only by the Church, but, more importantly, by the police—or possibly by someone high up in government?'

'The same source that provides him, by registered post, with regular and generous living expenses,' Judge Livi said.

'As I said, it's a labyrinth. But at the heart of it, there's Pierre Brossard. And that's why I'm here. Is it possible for you to give me that search warrant, without anyone but ourselves knowing about it?'

'This religious house,' Judge Livi said. 'Where is it located?'

'In Villefranche. I have the address.'

'Good.' Judge Livi leaned back and smiled. 'When my secretary goes to lunch, I'll type it up myself.'

CHAPTER TWENTY-ONE

Three Dutch tourists sat at a table beside the pool in the Novotel outside Aix, eating Cavaillon melons with white plastic spoons. T found fat people offensive, especially when they took their clothes off. He moved his sun umbrella around to block them from view. He was trying to read a *série noir policier* because, as he told Janine once, 'I like fairy-tales.' The *métier* was nothing like a *série noir*. There were no Inspector Maigrets in real life. There were guys like Pochon and who would write a *policier* about

145

Pochon? T was nervous. He had been waiting here since Friday afternoon when he phoned Pochon to tell him he'd lost Brossard. Now it was Sunday afternoon. No word. No new orders, nothing. He supposed they were still looking. He read a few more pages of the *policier*, then heard a church bell ring. All day long it had tolled out the hours. Five o'clock. Today was the day he had promised to phone Janine and tell her when he'd be back. His *fête* was Tuesday. No way now. Too bad. She'll be pissed off. She's been counting on it.

He'd left the air-conditioning on full when he went down to the pool at lunchtime, but his room wasn't cool when he went back up. He took off the hotel bathrobe and lay on the bed in his swimming trunks. Paris. He dialled her number.

'Hello, yes?' She sounded as if she'd been asleep.

'It's me. Are you OK?'

'I'm not OK. And you're a fucking liar. Where are you?'

'What do you mean I'm a liar?'

'Your father's not ill. Your father's dead.'

'Who told you that?'

'Your sister. Farah. She left a message and her number on your machine. I rang her. You never said you had a sister.'

'I hardly ever see her. She's a pain in the arse.'

'Are you in Bayeux? Don't lie to me, now.'

'No. I'm on a job. I've been held up. I rang to tell you to cancel the party for my *fête*. I can't make it Tuesday.'

'Where are you?'

'In Provence. OK?'

'Are you working for Muhammad? You'd better not be. You promised.'

146

'No. It's something else. Look, I'm protected on this one. That's all I can tell you, but it's the truth.'

'I ordered *sebas*, from that Arab *traiteur*, you know those little honey cakes you love. I told them enough for ten.'

'Why did you do that? I told you it wasn't certain. I told you I'd let you know if I could make it back in time.'

'Yes, from your father's sick bed. You bastard. I feel like a fool. I've already invited six people.'

'Janine, *chérie*, I'm sorry about this. Listen, do you remember that horoscope you read me? The one in *Elle*. I looked for *Elle* here in Aix but I can't find a copy. Do you still have yours?'

'So you're in Aix?'

'Never mind where I am. Do you have it?'

'I'll see.'

He heard her footsteps on the tiled floor of her kitchen. Then: 'Here we are. "Virgo. With a seventh house, Saturn, in your solar return chart—"'

'No, skip all that. It's the bit at the end.'

'Mmm ... "As Mars moves to Leo on the 9th you will be forced into an action that could do you great harm. If possible you should not agree to a proposal that others have made to you. This is no time to play the hero."'

'That's it,' he said. 'Tomorrow's the 9th. I just wanted to check.'

'Yes, well, you'd better watch out what you do tomorrow. The stuff just ahead of that was right. Listen: "You will have to make a sudden trip and lose out on previously planned pleasures." Dead on. No *sebas* for you.'

'I know,' he said. 'And it was very sweet of you to order them. What a pity. Listen, I love you. I'll try to

147

ring you Tuesday.'

'What am going to do with you?' she said. 'Anyway, take care. I love you too.'

One problem with the last two days was that he hadn't been able to leave the hotel for fear of missing Pochon's call. And the food in the dining room was shit. He had a feeling that Pochon might call that evening and he was right. A waiter came to his table at 9 p.m., just as he was finishing dessert. The waiter said there was a telephone booth in the alcove just outside the hotel dining room, but he didn't take the call there. He went up to his room.

Pochon's voice, cold and quiet. 'Ready? Got a pencil?'

'Yes, sir.'

'Villefranche. Or, to be exact, just outside Villefranche. An abbey on the Haute Corniche four kilometres above the Hôtel Bristol. The Bristol's a resort hotel, you can't miss it. The subject is driving there tomorrow, coming from Aix. He'll know your car.'

'I thought of that, sir. I've rented a smaller car. In the same name.'

'You can't rent a new face. He has a good memory.'

'Yes, sir, I know.'

'Remember, the paper must be pinned to the subject.'

'Of course.'

'Leave now.'

'Right, sir.'

148

CHAPTER TWENTY-TWO

When he sat down at the kitchen table, he saw that Nicole had left three *tartines* on his plate, buttered as in the old days. And a small pot of apricot jam. She knew he liked apricot jam. Last night she told him she'd have to catch the seven-thirty bus to La Napoule this morning in order to be at work at eight when the hotel guests started to leave. When he woke at first light he'd heard her moving about in the kitchen and then the old dog whimpering as she opened the door to leave. 'Poor Bobi, poor Bobi. Good boy. I'll be back tonight.'

He poured the coffee she had left on the stove. Those could be the last words I ever hear her say. I'll miss her. It was good, being in Cannes, wasn't it, a real *détente*, nobody in the whole wide world knowing where I am. Living in a flat like an ordinary person, having someone I know cook the things I like, getting pissed on good wine, instead of sleeping in a monastery guest house, eating monastery mush at a refectory table while some monk reads to us about the life of St Francis of Assisi.

He spread jam liberally on the *tartines*. Apricot jam and, yesterday, a *cassoulet* for lunch. Women don't forget these things. Even though she hates my guts she got them for me. Poor Nicole, she never understood. I didn't want to leave her. I *had* to leave her. They were after me, I couldn't live a normal life any more. And now, after all these years, she remembered my treats. Well, I have a treat for her. When she comes home tonight, I'll be gone. She can celebrate. She earned that Yid money fast. Only two days of putting up with me. It's funny. After all those years of scrabbling for every sou, now I don't even get to spend it, I have to pretend in every convent and monastery that I'm some sort of beggar, so that they'll have that holy feeling of doing their Christian duty in putting me up. It's a joke, eh? All I wanted after the war was a quiet life, Nicole, kids, who knows? And what did I get? A beggar's life at a monastery door.

Here he comes, yes, Bobi, I'm in here, in the kitchen, come on in, afraid of me, aren't you, boy? Stupid old dog. That's it, get in under the counter. Are you safe in there? You think I can't reach you? Well, we'll see. We'll see.

When he phoned the Commissaire yesterday he said he was in Aix and would leave this morning for Villefranche. Aix to Villefranche was a two-hour drive. He was supposed to phone the Commissaire when he got there. The Commissaire would expect a call around noon. But from Cannes Villefranche was just a short hop on the autoroute. No need to leave Cannes just yet. He decided to drive down to the Croisette, park the Peugeot and take a stroll along the front. He remembered his young days, dodging furtively among the parasols on the stony beach, trying to get up close to the girls lying on lilos, sunbathing.

Would he leave a note for Nicole? Yes. Don't keep her in suspense. He scribbled: *Goodbye. Thanks. P.* on the back of a pink wrapper she'd brought back yesterday from a local patisserie. In it, wrapped up and tied with a fancy ribbon, a *religieuse* and a *Napoléon*. His favourites. Who else knew or remembered what he liked? Nobody. My sister in La Rochelle, she doesn't even acknowledge that I exist.

150

No kids, no family. Nobody except Nicole who I had to ditch, is it any wonder she hates my guts? Nobody loves me, nobody cares. No, that's wrong. I have enemies, at least.

He put the note on the kitchen counter near the stove. She can't miss it there. The old dog crouched beneath the counter made the mistake of giving a frightened growl. He looked down into its blind eyes. What are you growling for? He took aim and neatly kicked Bobi in the throat. The dog choked, then howled. 'Shut up!' he said, in a voice that stilled the animal's howl at once. Obeyed, he went into the bedroom, packed his things and left, locking the door with his own key.

Cannes was a safe town, well, as safe as any town could be, now that he was a *cause célèbre*. When he parked the car and began his stroll along the Croisette, he wore his dark glasses and a hat. Resort towns like Cannes were full of tourists, people who didn't know each other. And the locals saw so many strange faces, they no longer noticed anyone. As for the tourists they were on the look-out for celebrities, it was film stars they had in mind, not a 'twice-condemned-to-death', whose last public photo was a police mug shot, forty years old.

And yet how safe was he here, how safe was he on any street? He walked along the Croisette, ignored by the touts promoting sightseeing tours, by street photographers offering to take a souvenir snapshot, by homeless adolescents begging for change. He was not a source of money for any of these. He did not look like a tourist, a pensioner, perhaps, invisible, particularly to the young who, here on holiday, did not want to be reminded of the leprosy of age. And yet it could happen, he was always at risk, a *flic*, or

151

someone who remembered his photo, even someone from the past.

As he came to the great seafront hotels he heard, in a back street, the tolling of a church carillon. He stopped, facing the sea, the sun hot on his cheeks. He shut his eyes and said a prayer. 'O Lord, protect me, save me, grant me eternal rest.' I must pray more, I must go to mass each day, I must be always in the state of grace. I am old. My time is short. And the Jews want my hide. They could be waiting for me now in Villefranche. I should go somewhere new.

He opened his eyes and stared at the sea. I have money, I can live for months, live in comfort. I don't have to pick up the Paris payment or the Chevaliers', for that matter. Well, not for a while. I could throw the Jews off the scent, take a flight to Paris today. By tomorrow I could be in some place like Rouen or Coutances. Somewhere I never go.

But even as he let these thoughts enter his mind he knew he could not do it. He would have to tell the Commissaire, and the Commissaire would veto it. The Commissaire had said, time and time again, that the Church should be his hiding place, that nowhere else would he be so safe. Especially now when the police are no longer on my case. Besides, if I run off to Normandy without telling the Commissaire that's the end of his help for me. No, I have to go on.

He turned away from the sea. The carillon ended its peal. He shivered in the sun. Those bells. A funeral sound.

CHAPTER TWENTY-THREE

When T drove along the winding road that leads from the Nice-Monaco highway down to the port and resort village of Villefranche, it was night and he was worried. It was the beginning of the season. The hotels would be full. And they were. He was turned away, first from the Welcome on the seafront, then from the Versailles, the Bahía and the Provençal. It was after midnight when he found a room in a mean little place in a back alley in the narrow old streets behind the seafront. He hated such places. They drowned him again in a memory of Sète, and his childhood. No toilet in the room, no shower, no *télé*, nothing. A single bed, with a deep groove in its lumpy mattress where a thousand travellers had tossed and turned, as he did, all night long.

He had left his car in a car-park off the Place St Michel, halfway up the village. He rose in the pre-dawn dark, shaved and dressed under a miserable single light bulb in the dirty bathroom at the end of the corridor, and walked up to the square where the cafés were just beginning to set up their outdoor tables and chairs. As he approached, a waiter sluiced water on the pavement. The pavement steamed. The sun was already hot. There was a kiosk next door to the café he chose. It offered newspapers, fan magazines, postcards and maps. He asked for a detailed local map. As he paid, he saw a stack of *Nice Matins* on the counter. He did not read the headline: he read the date. *Monday May 9, 1989*.

He sat at an outdoor table with a coffee and brioche. The map showed the Haute Corniche, above the Nice-Monaco highway. T left the brioche half eaten, paid his bill, reclaimed his car from the underground *parking* at Place St Michel and drove out, following the map. Ten minutes later he passed the Hôtel Bristol, four kilometres from the priory. The Haute Corniche road was lined with elegant villas, hidden behind stone walls and groves of trees: quiet, no shops. But he could see this wasn't the place to do it. Already, there was a constant coming and going of traffic, delivery trucks, private cars and tour buses. As the day wore on, the traffic would increase.

The priory came into view at last. Behind eight-foot-high stone walls a red-tiled roof rose up above a frieze of plane trees. There was no sign, other than a rusting iron cross, at right-angles to the entrance. There was nowhere to park without being seen, but he took a chance and drove on for a further fifty yards. He was in luck. A little opening at a bend of the road had a sign saying: *Vista Point*. A perfect place to lie in wait. He turned the car round so that it faced the priory entrance and sat staring at the heavy wooden gates. *May 9*. A horoscope's a warning, isn't it? I mean, it's telling you what you'd better do and what you'd better not do. It's telling you when your luck's in and when it's out. It doesn't mean that some fucking disaster is going to happen to me today, not that, it's telling me that on the 9th I'll be forced into an action that could hurt me. It said *if possible* I shouldn't go along with a proposal that others made to me. *If possible*. What's that mean? Doesn't mean I should walk off the job, does it? No, it's a warning, yes, that's it, a *warning*. And the warning says, *if possible* today's not the day to do it. So, listen. If the subject turns up this morning and books in down the road, all I have to do is to heed the warning. Keep

154

him in my sights. Follow him if he goes out today, but don't *do it* today. Tomorrow's the 10th. Wait till tomorrow.

But again, he remembered that rich old Jew in his St Germain apartment, heard again that quiet voice: *You must kill him on your first attempt. You may not get a second chance.* And he's seen me, already. Seventy years old, but he's quick. Oh fuck. It's only a horoscope. Some stupid bitch wrote it up in her office, what does she know?

Still. *This is no time to play the hero.*

CHAPTER TWENTY-FOUR

When Captain Daniel Dumesnil came back to his office, just before lunch hour on the morning of May the 9th, Sergeant Picot handed him a slip of paper. 'A Colonel Roux called from Paris, sir. He left this number. He asks if you can call him straightaway. A private matter, he said.'

'When did he call?'

'Ten-thirty, sir.'

He went into his office and shut the door. Private. I wonder? Robert is in charge of the Brossard affair.

He picked up the phone. A voice he had known since their training days: 'Roux.'

'Robert, it's Daniel.'

'Daniel, how are you? How are the kids?'

'Fine, fine. And Claire?'

'She's in great form. She sends her love. And to Martine. Look, I'm coming your way.'

'When?'

'This afternoon. And I need your help.

Specifically, I need four of your best men for two or three days. And transport.'

'What's happening?'

'I'll tell you when I see you. In the meantime, I don't want anyone, and I mean anyone, to know I'm in Nice or why. Now. Can you fix me up?'

'I'll give you two of my sergeant-majors, and two corporals. They're the best.'

'Great. I need them now. Is that possible?'

'Yes.'

'I want you to send two of them to stake out a location in Villefranche. It's a priory of the Carmelite Order on the Haute Corniche road. The person I'm looking for is old, probably driving a 1977 white Peugeot.'

'Monsieur Pierre?'

'Right. You have a photo on file. Show it to your men. If anyone who seems to fit that description comes out of the priory I want him followed. Out of town, wherever. They mustn't lose him. Remember he's a Houdini. And they must tell nobody, and I mean nobody, who it is they're watching. Can you start the stakeout now? Our man may be on his way there today.'

Dumesnil looked at his watch. 'If I'm to use my best team, I've got to take them off other jobs. I can't guarantee a start before two o'clock.'

He heard Roux hesitate, then: 'Two o'clock will be fine. Our man may not surface before then and if he does, he's likely to go to ground in the priory. I'm on my way. If you start the stakeout at two, I hope we can get inside the priory by four. Villefranche is, what? Ten minutes from Nice?'

'Seven kilometres.'

156

'Good. And remember, Daniel. We're walking on eggs.'

'Church property. Right of asylum. All that?'

'Yes. But I have a search warrant.'

CHAPTER TWENTY-FIVE

The priory of St Michel des Monts on the Haute Corniche above Villefranche, had, until 1930, been called the Villa Del Lago. In that year its owner, a textiles millionaire, died and willed his property to the Carmelite Order. The house, a thirty-room mansion in the Mediterranean style, was surrounded by two acres of formal gardens and the property included riding stables and a swimming pool. The Carmelites converted the stables into a chapel and erected a cross over the roof but left the villa untouched. It now housed eighteen contemplative monks, under the direction of a prior, Dom Henri Arminjon, a native of Nantes, who was the author of several works on mystical theology. The Carmelite Order, following the wishes of the villa's late owner, opened its doors four times yearly for two-week retreat periods, which were planned especially for businessmen.

Now, as he drove his little white Peugeot through the entrance gates, he hoped that no retreat was in progress. For, in that case, he would be obliged to stay out of sight in the gardener's cottage at the end of the estate. However, retreat, or not, this was one place he was sure of a welcome. The Prior, a dignified and distant figure, intimidated him, but was a man he could look up to, revered by the Chevaliers as a saint in the making.

And so, cruising the little Peugeot along the gravelled drive which led to the pink splendour of the mansion, he began to hope that here, at last, he might risk a longer stay.

The *père hospitalier*, whose name he did not remember, came down the marble steps, smiling, waving to him.

'Monsieur Pierre! How are you?'

'Hello, Father.' He got out of the car and they shook hands. 'How nice to be here again. Your garden is beautiful this year. Are you having a retreat?'

'Not at the moment. But our next one starts the day after tomorrow. So, I'm afraid I can't put you up in the main house. It will have to be the gardener's cottage.'

He smiled gratefully at the priest. 'Oh, God bless you, Father, that will be perfect. And more private, if you know what I mean.'

'Yes, indeed. I must tell Father Joseph you're here. It's just a formality, I'm sure, but he would want to know. Our Prior is in Rome at the moment, so Father Joseph is in charge.'

The gardener's cottage was at the far end of the estate in the middle of a vegetable garden. He took the key which the *père hospitalier* had given him and unlocked the door. A small grass snake lay immobile on the stone step leading up to the sitting room. He turned and went back to his car to get the car jack as a killing tool. But when he returned the snake was gone. This incident reminded him that he was not armed. After what happened in Salon I should carry a gun at all times, even in the safety of this place.

He took the revolver from the glove compartment of the car and put it in the deep pocket of his

158

overblouse, then laboriously carried his three suitcases into the cottage. The last suitcase, containing his mementoes, was so heavy that he had difficulty lifting it up the steps. It was not locked and now he opened it and stared at its contents: Iron Crosses, Afrika Corps caps, SS insignia, Nazi flags and banners. I no longer need the money I used to make from these. The sensible thing would be to get in touch with that dealer in Lille. Kids find this stuff romantic. Offer him the lot at an overall price. Sell it to the skinheads, that's what he'll do. Fair enough.

He heard a noise outside, shut the lid of the box, went to the window and looked down the rows of vegetables. A monk, his long, clay-coloured robe hiked up to his knees, was hoeing near the compost heap. He saw the monk straighten up, as a wooden gate creaked open and Father Joseph Cartier came into the vegetable garden.

Joseph. Coming to see me?

The almoner of the priory, Father Joseph, had been his classmate at the beginning of the thirties in the St François de Salles day school in Toulon. Their fathers, sergeants in the regular army, had served in the same regiment in World War I, and were devoted readers of *L'Action Française*. Both had enrolled their sons in the Catholic boy scout movement, both were vociferous denunciators of the corruption of the Third Republic by Jews, freemasons and communists. Because of all this, he and Joseph Cartier should have been like brothers. Yet they had not been best friends. And now, as he watched him come up the path to the cottage, he could not be sure that Joseph was on his side. The Prior was his protector in this house. Joseph, shy and distant, seemed in every sense a contemplative, frail, taciturn,

159

his mind turned towards God.

But it was Joseph he would have to deal with today. He went to the door of the cottage, opened it and came out into the sunlight, smiling, his hand extended in welcome. Joseph either did not see this gesture or ignored it, bowing his head slightly in greeting, his hands remaining deep in the folds of his habit.

'Ah, Pierre.'

'So you're in charge now, Joseph,' he said. 'What does that feel like?' He laughed, to show that this was not a serious question. But Joseph chose to answer it.

'It's a responsibility I'd prefer to avoid. Especially now that you're here.'

Joseph turned and looked back down the rows of the vegetable garden. The monk, hoeing there, was out of earshot.

'We'll be starting a retreat here, the day after tomorrow,' Joseph said. 'There will be strangers, laymen, in the grounds. It's perhaps not a good time for you to visit.'

So that's it. The Cardinal's men have talked to him. 'I know,' he said. 'But I'll stay out of sight, I promise you. To be honest, though, I have very few choices left. Last week, the Jews sent someone to murder me. I was spared, thank God. But our enemies are closing in on me. I need friends, as never before.'

He waited, watching Joseph. That instinct that had never failed him in the past did not fail him now. Joseph had turned against him.

'Our Prior, as you know, is presently in Rome,' Joseph said. 'I don't expect him back for another week. Therefore I'll have to make this decision myself.'

160

'Of course. But, as you know, Dom Henri has always supported me. We share the same beliefs about the state of the world. I'm sure he wouldn't refuse me now.'

'I think you're right,' Joseph said. 'And because I'm acting on his behalf, I don't feel that I have the right to refuse you, either. I say this, despite the fact that I know it's against the wishes of Cardinal Delavigne that we shelter you. I don't like to be put in a position of disobeying the Cardinal. But before he left for Rome Dom Henri mentioned the Cardinal's request and said he didn't agree with it. Neither he nor I guessed that you would be arriving so soon on our doorstep. The question for me now is what would Dom Henri say to you, knowing that a retreat will start in two days' time. Would he limit your visit to the next two days?'

When they turn against you, there's no going back. But why let him get away with it? 'Joseph, I'll help you with that decision. If you're unhappy with my being here while the retreat is in progress, I will, of course, leave before then. It's sad, though, that this decision comes from my old classmate, whose father was so close to mine, we who were brought up in the same way.'

'Yes, we were brought up in the same way,' Joseph said. 'We're both children of the Church as it was in France when we were boys. It was a Church that saw modern society as an insult against God's laws, a Church that was anti-democratic, filled with clerics and laymen who would think of you as the victim of a plot by those Jews, freemasons, communists, whom we were taught to fear and despise. It is that Church that still claims your allegiance and which, by shielding you, forgives you and, in doing so, forgives

161

itself for its silence when thousands of Jews were sent to their deaths.'

'Why are you so bitter, Joseph? I don't remember *you* helping any Jews.'

'You're right. I chose to become a monk, to turn away from the world and give my life to God. But what did that mean? Did God give me permission to ignore what was happening here? How could it be right to turn away, when in doing so, I was betraying France?'

'What are you talking about? Betraying France?'

'My silence was a betrayal. Unlike you, I didn't believe in Vichy or Pétain. I felt ashamed that France had willingly become the Nazis' servant state. But I did nothing. I said nothing.'

'And the communists—was that the side you should have picked, their armies raping women, running wild through Europe, their Jew commissars bringing us the teachings of a godless state?'

'Pierre, listen to me. I've heard you express your opinions when you came here in the past. You've never showed any contrition for the killings you committed in the *milice*. On the contrary you continually justify your actions. You pretend to be devout, you pretend to have found God, and I know you've managed to convince many priests, even those who despise what you did, that during the war you acted in good faith. You've deceived them, but you cannot deceive God.'

'So you're turning me out. Pushing me into the arms of the Jews who are trying to murder me. All right. But stop giving me a lecture. You're just trying to excuse yourself. You're afraid of me, now that I'm hunted, now that I'm a *cause célèbre*. Admit it. And don't tell me that God hasn't forgiven me. How do

162

you know?'

'That's true. I'm sorry.'

'All right, then. I have only one question for you. I want to stay here tonight. I must make arrangements. I must find out if the next place where I ask for asylum will, unlike you, treat me with the charity and forgiveness the Church has always shown to men like me.'

Father Joseph bowed his head, then said, 'Very well. You may stay here tonight.'

Then turned away, walking back up the path, past the monk hoeing near the compost heap. The wooden gate of the vegetable garden squealed as Joseph opened it. In the stables that had been converted into a chapel, a bell tolled. The gardener monk put aside his hoe, made the sign of the cross and stood, silent in prayer. At the garden gate Father Joseph also crossed himself and bowed his head to pray.

He watched them both. The Angelus bell. The prayer at noon. The Commissaire expects me to ring him around now. But not from here. I'll call from the town.

* * *

Five minutes later, the *père hospitalier*, sitting in his office under the *porte cochère* of the mansion, saw the little Peugeot come up the drive, approaching the main gates. He pressed the electric gate opener and the heavy iron gates swung wide. When the Peugeot reached the Corniche road outside it stopped, although no traffic was passing by.

Fifty yards up the road, a vista point. Three tourist cars were parked there. Half a dozen tourists, armed with cameras, were taking pictures of each other against the panorama below. It looked harmless but he took care to identify the makes of all three cars, before driving off in the direction of Villefranche.

You cannot deceive God. Why did he say that, Joseph? Because he has always been on the other side, a Jew lover. I might have known it. In all the times I've come here over the years, he's never wanted to talk about our early days. Now, I know why. *You cannot deceive God.* I'm not trying to deceive God! Jesus, my Saviour, I pray to You, I worship You, I could never deceive You. I didn't deceive anyone, not Monsignor Le Moyne, not Abbé Feren, I confessed my faults and was given absolution. He's wrong. Joseph, he'll never understand. Contrition for what I did in the *milice*? What I did in the *milice* was right for the time, right for the war we were fighting. Why do I let him upset me, I feel faint, I feel my heart. I've got to talk to the Commissaire. Things are bad now, worse than ever. Maybe it's the moment to ask the Commissaire if he can get me out. Bolivia, he said. But that was years ago. Still he always wanted me to leave France.

Villefranche was like a second home. The old town behind the seafront, with its narrow streets and alleys, was the dark heart of the port, a brothel quarter in the years when the American fleet called here, hidden away from the tourists who strolled along the marine promenade and ate in the waterfront restaurants. He had been a guest in the priory so many times in the past twenty years that he knew every street in the old town. He had his regular café in the Rue Obscure, a place where he was known, but not known, a place where he had often picked up his envelope. There was a closed telephone kiosk in

164

the rear of the café.

Now, as he came down on to the lower Corniche road above Villefranche, he looked again and again in his rear-view mirror, just to be sure. The third time he looked he saw a green Renault Clio. One of the cars at the Vista Point had been a green Renault Clio. Could be coincidence. He turned into the upper reaches of Villefranche and drove down towards the seafront. Suddenly, he swung into the kerb and parked. The green Clio went past, headed for the yacht basin. He drove on. In the underground *parking* at Place St Michel he locked the Peugeot and walked down a steep narrow street, leading to the dark alley known as the Rue Obscure. He still felt faint. His mouth was dry and he was hungry. After I call the Commissaire, I'll have a beer and some food.

But what about the call to the Commissaire: will I say it? Will I, at last, get my Vatican passport? Will I end my days in some bugridden, half-black country, sitting in a stinking café surrounded by greasy *métèques*? What choice do I have? Even with the Chevaliers helping me, there are only a few places that will take me now. And most of them are '*intégriste*' with mealtime readings and prayer vigils and no television. At least, in another country I could relax, live in an apartment, eat what I want when I want it. What should I do, should I test the waters and ask about a passport? Will that make him angry?

He was passing familiar shops, bars, vegetable stalls, coming into the darkness of the Rue Obscure. Half-way up the street was the Bar Les Antilles with its beaded front curtain, its little-used outdoor tables and, inside, a row of banquettes, an old-fashioned football machine and a little zinc bar adjoining the kitchen. He pushed aside the curtain and went into

165

the gloom. There were only four customers, two old men playing draughts, and, in one of the banquettes, an alcoholic couple, man and wife, silent over tumblers of Ricard. At the zinc counter, Max Pellan, the proprietor, was reading the sports pages of *Nice Matin*. He looked up, his reading glasses slipping to the tip of his empurpled nose. 'Ah, Monsieur Pierre. How's it going? Back for a visit?'

'Just a short one, this time.'

They shook hands. 'What can I offer you, Monsieur Pierre?'

'I've been thinking about *pan bagnat*. Do you have it today?'

Max looked into the little kitchen behind the bar where his wife was chopping onions.

'Clotilde? *Pan bagnat*, is it possible?'

'Yes.'

Max turned back, pushing his glasses up on his nose. 'And to drink, Monsieur Pierre?'

'A beer. But first I must make a phone call. Can you let me have a *jeton*?'

Max reached into a tin box and handed him two phone counters. 'Go ahead.'

Just beyond the zinc bar, a corridor led to the phone kiosk which faced the door of the toilet. At the end of the corridor was a locked and barred back entrance. He entered the phone kiosk and, pulling its folding glass partition shut behind him, stood, trying to get up his courage. The passport, yes, or no? What will he say?

He dialled Avignon.

'Hello, yes?'

'Monsieur Pierre here, Madame. Is your husband at home?'

'One moment, please.'

166

As he waited, he glanced through the glass panel in the direction of the bar. No one coming through. Take it easy. Why should I be afraid of him?

'Hello?'

The Commissaire's voice. And at once it was as though the years had fallen away like leaves from a tree and he again faced someone he was afraid of, someone like Commandant Lecussan in the days of the *milice*. Men like this had the gift of giving fear. And he who could charm abbots and monsignors had never had a chance with the Commissaire who had always treated him as someone whose silence had been bought, who could be destroyed at will. And now he must ask a great favour of this man.

'It's me, sir. I promised to telephone you when I arrived in Villefranche.'

'You're there already?'

'Yes, sir. But I'm afraid there's a problem. The priory will only accept me for one night.'

'*What?*' The Commissaire's voice was suddenly loud.

'There's a laymen's religious retreat starting there in two days' time. Besides, I think they're afraid. The Cardinal's men have been talking to them.'

'But you'll be staying there tonight?'

'Yes, sir.'

'And then?'

'Tomorrow I'll move to Nice. I don't see any problem in Nice. Dom Olivier is Prior General and a great friend of the Chevaliers.'

As he spoke, he heard footsteps behind him in the corridor. He turned and saw a kid in a blue anorak and an American baseball cap go into the toilet and close the door. He did not see the kid's face.

'Yes, I know Dom Olivier,' the Commissaire said.

167

'You should be safe there. Phone me tomorrow as soon as you arrive.'

He hesitated, cradling the receiver between his shoulder and his ear, as he turned to look back at the shut toilet door. Who's that kid? This is what I'm up against. I can't turn my back, day or night. I've got to get away.

'Sir, there *is* a problem. I can't stay in Nice for long. Even in those circles, word could get out. I'll have to move on very soon. Sir, I think it's time for a change of plan. I'd like to go abroad.'

There was silence in Avignon. He tried again.

'Some time ago, sir, you urged me to take this step. Do you remember?'

'That was years ago.'

'But is it still possible, sir? I think it would be best for all concerned, don't you?'

'I have no opinion on that,' the Commissaire said. He did not sound angry, which was a blessing. 'I'll have to think about it. In the meantime, remember, we're paying you, we're protecting you. You do your part and we'll do ours. Relax. We'll work something out.'

'But, to be honest, sir, I can't relax, not for a moment, sir. After all, they've tried to kill me twice, first in Salon and then in Aix. My life's in danger as never before.'

'If I were you I'd stop worrying,' the Commissaire said. 'You gave that second one the slip, didn't you? Listen to me. I haven't told you yet, but the police now know who these people are. They're working on it. I don't think you'll have to worry much longer.'

Could he believe him? Were they just trying to keep him from losing his nerve? 'If you're right, sir, that's very good news.'

168

'Of course I'm right! Phone me tomorrow.'

'Yes, sir. Thank you, sir.'

He heard the Commissaire hang up. He stood for a moment, trying to fix the exact words of the conversation. Nowadays, unbelievably, he often forgot what had been said, he who in the old days was known as the Recording Angel of the Second Section. The Commissaire didn't say no. He had not been angry. 'I'll have to think about it.' That's what he said. He'll have to do more than think about it. I can't go on like this. Never mind about them finding those Jews, it's the gendarmerie who's on my tail now, there's no stopping those army bastards, or that *juge d'instruction*, that Jewess looking for revenge. Bolivia, somewhere, anywhere, would be better than this.

He came out of the kiosk and went back to the zinc bar. A tall cool glass of beer had been placed at the end of the counter and, beside it, a paper napkin and a knife and fork. Max, marking his selection on the racing page, moistened the tip of his pencil with his tongue and said, as if to himself, 'Athos.'

He sat down at the counter and said to Max, 'Athos?'

'Three o'clock at Auteuil,' Max said. 'I have a feeling about that horse. Clotilde?'

'Coming.'

Madame Pellan, thin and stooped, came from the small kitchen carrying the *pan bagnat* sandwich on a plate surrounded by black olives.

'I've been dreaming of that,' he told her. 'Yours is the best *pan bagnat* in all of Provence.'

'Thank you. *Bon appetit*, Monsieur Pierre.'

He took a bite of the sandwich. Tuna, olive oil, tomatoes, in a hollowed-out roll. Easy on his

169

dentures. I won't get any *pan bagnat* if I move to some *métèque* country. Knab's in Argentina now, under the name of Heller. Vatican passport. But that was in the days of Pius XII. This Pope's a Polack, going around the world like a salesman, celebrating mass with bare-arsed savages and making cardinals out of niggers. Still, even if the Vatican can't help now, Commissaire Vionnet has influence. He works for the Prefect. Ex-Prefect now. It's all influence, who you are, who you were. They talk about justice but the charges against me and Monsieur le Préfet are exactly the same, crime against humanity, yet he's never had to run, lives in a big apartment in Paris, invited to state receptions, sees his grandchildren every week, not to worry if you're him, with *juge* after *juge d'instruction* putting his case aside, year after year.

'*Salut!*'

A new customer pushed aside the beaded front curtain and waved to Max. Middle-aged, a regular, by the sound of him. He watched him sit in the banquette next to the alcoholics. Max, without being asked, took up a bottle of Ricard, poured a measure, then brought the glass and a carafe of water to the man's table.

'What's new, Max? Got something for today?' the man said.

'Athos. Three o'clock. Auteuil.'

The customer shrugged. '*Boh!*'

'Well, you asked,' Max said. He went back behind the bar.

The *pan bagnat* was eaten and he was spitting out the stone of the last olive when he thought of the toilet. That kid never came out. All at once, he felt the hackle of danger. He asked Max.

'Listen, is it possible to go out through the back way?'

Max shook his head.

'You sure?'

'Of course. If there was a way out, I'd be robbed blind. They'd go down to the toilet and disappear.'

It must be fifteen minutes or more since the kid went in. Too long. He turned and looked back down the corridor. What he saw there made him get off his bar stool. The toilet door was ajar. If it's him, is he watching me now? Making sure I haven't left? If it's him, he lost me in Aix. He'll be worried about that.

Relax, the Commissaire said. But how does he expect me to relax? He didn't say they'd *caught* these Jews. Be sensible. There's a kid in the toilet, maybe he's taking a hit. But the door was closed when I came out of the kiosk. Why is it not closed now?

He knew what he must do. He said to Max, loud enough to be heard back there, 'Give me a *jeton*, will you? I have to make another phone call.'

He put his hand into his blouse as he walked down the corridor towards the telephone booth. He looked, not at the booth, but at the toilet door lying slightly ajar. When he reached the booth he hesitated, then, as if changing his mind, turned and pushed open the toilet door. The toilet was old-fashioned, tiled, filthy, dating from fifty years ago, a hole in the ground, with no toilet seat. Standing with his back to him, pretending to piss into the hole, was the kid in the American baseball cap. He could not see the kid's face.

'Sorry,' he said. 'You didn't shut the door.'

'No problem,' the kid said. He did not turn around.

He stood, watching the kid's back. There was no

171

urine going into the hole in the floor. There was no sign of a needle. He slipped his revolver half out of his blouse.

'Will you be long?' he asked.

He saw the kid stiffen and pretend to shake his prick dry. He saw the kid's right arm go up, not to zip his fly, but into the anorak. That was it. He knew, although he'd not seen the kid's face. At the moment the kid reached into the anorak for his gun, he shot him twice in the back. He watched him fall on his knees on the urine-soaked tiles. The kid's gun made a clatter as it dropped beside the toilet hole. He went closer, pulled up the head and saw the dying face. It was the one from Aix.

The noise of two shots had been loud in the bar. Max's footsteps, coming, running. He stuffed his own gun back in his blouse and went to the toilet door.

'I was in the phone booth,' he told Max. 'I think it's a suicide.'

Max, shaken, went into the toilet. Within seconds Max would know the truth.

He ran down the corridor, through the café, and into the Rue Obscure. His heart hammering in his chest, he ran down the street, then down the flight of steps that led to the waterfront, coming out into an anonymity of strolling tourists, out to the sunlight, the silver glitter of the sea.

CHAPTER TWENTY-SIX

It was an official jeep, unmistakably gendarmerie: its driver, Sergeant Picot, armed with an automatic weapon, as was the corporal who sat beside him. In

172

the rear, alone, his impeccable uniform clearly showing his rank as lieutenant-colonel, Roux sat, a briefcase on his knees, his overnight bag at his feet. He had arranged to be picked up directly at Nice airport and driven straight to Villefranche. Now, as they rounded the last bend on the Haute Corniche road, he could see the heavy gates of the priory of St Michel des Monts ahead, its rusted iron cross slightly askew to the right of the entrance. Where was the stakeout?

And then he saw a gendarmerie jeep parked in the little circle of the Vista point. In its front seats a sergeant and a corporal, both in uniform.

'Those our men?'

'Yes, sir.'

'Dammit, I asked for a stakeout, not a roadblock!'

'Sir?'

'Uniforms! Army vehicle! If the suspect saw that when he drove up here, he's long gone by now.'

'Sir.'

'Call them. Bring them here.'

When the stakeout jeep drove alongside, he leaned out. 'When did you men arrive?'

'Fourteen-ten hours, sir.'

'All right. Follow us in.'

The *père hospitalier* answered the gate telephone. 'Priory. Yes?'

'Gendarmerie. Will you open, please?'

As the two vehicles drove up to the *porte cochère*, the *père hospitalier* telephoned Father Joseph in his office.

'The police, Father. Two jeeps.'

'Where is our friend?'

'He went out a few hours ago. He hasn't come back yet. What will I say to them, Father?'

173

'Wait. I'll be down in a moment.'

The *père hospitalier*, Father Francis, went out on to the drive. 'What can I do for you, gentlemen?'

'Is there a rear entrance, Father?'

'Yes. At the other end of the grounds, past the chapel.'

'Sergeant, get down there. Corporal, you come with us.'

The stakeout jeep, accelerating, drove off in the direction of the stables. Roux, followed by Sergeant Picot and the two corporals, entered the main hallway of the mansion.

'Who's in charge here, Father?'

'Father Joseph. He's just coming.'

Descending the pink marble staircase was an elderly monk. He nodded politely in greeting as he crossed the ornate chequerboard tiles of the hall. 'Good afternoon, gentlemen.'

'I am Colonel Roux. This is a search warrant for these premises.'

Father Joseph took the typewritten sheet of paper and read it slowly. 'Pierre Brossard?' he said, at last.

'Yes. Is he here?'

'No, he is not.'

'But you know him?'

'Indeed, I do. We were boys at school together.'

'Then you know that he's wanted on the charge of a crime against humanity.'

'Yes.'

'He has stayed here in the past?'

'Our Prior, Dom Henri, is in Rome at the moment. I am acting for him in his absence, but because I am not the Prior, I don't feel it's within my competence to answer your question. As you know, Colonel, the Church's law of asylum supersedes, in the minds of

174

my superiors, the laws of the civil authority.'

'The search warrant you are holding is a legal document. It has nothing to do with the right of asylum. We are trying to find and arrest a criminal wanted on a capital charge. We are going to make a search here.'

Father Joseph nodded. 'In that case, Father Francis will show you through the house. Good day to you, gentlemen.' He turned to Father Francis. 'If you need me I will be in my study.'

'Yes, Father.'

The search began in the large ground-floor reception rooms. Roux saw half a dozen robed figures pacing the loggia outside, heads bent in prayer or meditation. The loggia with its stone pillars could have been the cloister of a monastery, had it not faced a large Riviera-style swimming pool surrounded by poolside beach umbrellas and plastic lounging chairs. As the search continued through the dining rooms and the mansion's kitchens, he was struck by the incongruity of a monastic community living in this setting of worldly affluence. And yet, the very presence of these monks had transformed and humbled the luxurious furniture, the ornate tiles, the wall sconces, the *boiserie*. The stone flower urns were empty in their niches, the walls were marked with yellowing spaces where paintings and mirrors had been removed. Affixed to the great bare wall of the landing leading to the first-floor rooms was an ugly modern statue of Jesus on the Cross, the Christ head hanging down as though in shame at being found in these surroundings.

Quickly, Roux directed his forces, each man moving along a different corridor as door after door was opened on empty bedrooms. They moved up to

175

the small servants' rooms on the third floor which were now monks' cells. He noticed that, during their searches, Father Francis did not behave like a man who had something to hide. When they had finished in the mansion, the priest led them out to the stables that had been converted into the priory's chapel. Roux, from habit and respect, dipped his hand into the Holy Water font and made the sign of the cross as he entered the nave. Two monks were kneeling in a vigil at the main altar. He gestured to Sergeant Picot who quickly made a tour of the sacristy and returned, signalling that he had found nothing.

When they came out of the chapel into the sunlight, one of the corporals came down from the loft above the old stables. Again, nothing.

'Any other rooms?' Roux asked and saw the *père hospitalier* hesitate.

'There are some sheds at the other end of the vegetable garden. Tools, pesticide, that sort of thing.'

'Let's have a look.'

Again, he saw the priest hesitate.

'This way, then.'

Ahead, as they walked quickly down through the rows of vegetables, Roux saw, near the toolsheds, a building that seemed to be a small cottage. 'What's that, Father?'

'It was the gardener's cottage. We use it now and then during retreats when we have an overflow of guests.'

At the end of the garden, beyond the cottage, Roux saw the stakeout jeep guarding the gate of the rear entrance. He went up the path to the cottage. The door was locked. 'Do you have a key, Father?'

'I—I'm afraid one of the other monks must have it. Father Paul has been using this place to store potting soil.'

'Can you get the key from him?'

'I'm afraid not, not at the moment. He's the one who would have it and he's in Nice today, buying supplies for tomorrow's retreat.'

Roux looked at Sergeant Picot who nodded, and went to the window of the cottage. Picot took out a knife, slid it under the window catch, then lifted the sash. He turned to the youngest corporal. 'René, you can get through here, can't you?'

The corporal wriggled through the narrow space. A moment later the door was open and Roux stood in the small living room, looking at three heavy suitcases and a small, worn leather trunk.

'Whose are these, Father?'

Again, he saw Father Francis hesitate. 'I'm not sure. Father Paul looks after this place.'

Roux signalled to Sergeant Picot. The suitcases were not locked. The first two contained male clothing, some prayer books, holy pictures and a much-used missal. And then Picot opened the largest suitcase. 'Sir? Look here.'

Roux bent over the suitcase, then glanced back at Father Francis. The priest seemed astonished. Roux lifted out an SS deaths' head insignia, then a Waffen SS motor-cycle flag. 'Whose are these?'

'I—I have no idea. I had no idea they were— Colonel, I think I had better get Father Joseph.'

'Do that, Father. And remember, I don't want you or anyone else to pick up a telephone. Is that understood?'

The priest nodded and went out. Roux hunkered down in front of the small leather trunk. It was locked over a leather flap. He cut the flap off with his knife. The trunk was neatly stacked with cardboard

177

files. 'Corporal, get this up on the table. Sergeant, search the garage and grounds. You're looking for a white Peugeot, late seventies vintage.'

When the sergeant went out, Roux sat down at the table. The first files told him everything. In the minutes in which he looked them over, waiting for Father Joseph to reappear, Roux realized that these were the record of forty years of effort to reverse the judgments of history and revoke the sentences imposed by the state.

*   *   *

At no time in all his years as a Carmelite monk had Joseph faced such a decision and felt so alone. It was as though this life that he had chosen, a life which, at the hour of his death, he might one day look back on with humility and gratitude, now seemed selfish and false. His years of prayer and self-denial, those years in which he had felt himself blessed with the joy of God's love, had they been simply a turning away from his duty to his fellow man? He who had, from his boyhood, distrusted the political beliefs of his father and Sergeant Brossard, who had served twenty years under a conservative superior like Dom Henri, had he not in some sense condoned the actions of such men? As later, in the post-war period of change within the Church he remained silent when Dom Henri criticized those South American priests and nuns who fought for and suffered with the poor and the oppressed. This afternoon as gendarmes searched through the rooms of the priory, threatening the peace of the community left in his charge, he must face, at last, the ultimate consequence of his failure to speak out. To speak now, or to remain silent? To tell
178

that colonel, yes, Brossard is staying here, he is not in the house at present but he will be back later, he plans to spend the night with us. He is a war criminal, a man I knew when we were boys, a person I have never trusted, a liar, a scoundrel. Arrest him.

Or again, to say nothing, neither helping nor hindering their efforts? To say nothing is to pretend I know nothing. Which is a lie. Which must I obey? My conscience or the rule of the Order? Alas, I know the answer. I cannot act selfishly to salve my conscience. To obey Dom Henri is to follow our rule, the rule by which we pledge obedience to God. I am a Carmelite monk. I must protect the Order against the scandal of Brossard's arrest in this house.

*   *   *

'Father Joseph?'

Francis, out of breath, worried.

'Yes, Francis.'

'They've found his luggage. It's in the cottage. The first suitcase they opened was full of Nazi stuff.'

'Nazi stuff?'

'Flags, armbands, medals—he must have collected them. I said I would fetch you. The Colonel said we're not to use the telephone.'

'Who does he think he is?' Joseph said. 'All right. Come with me.'

When they reached the cottage, Colonel Roux was at the kitchen table, examining the contents of cardboard file folders. A small leather trunk sat by his elbow. The suitcase of Nazi trash, Joseph saw at once, on the floor near the door. The Colonel looked up at Joseph. 'These are Pierre Brossard's belongings, Father. Where is his car?'

'I don't know,' Joseph said.

The Colonel turned to Francis. 'Do *you*?'

Father Francis hesitated and looked at Joseph.

'I am afraid we can't help you,' Joseph said.

'Is he on the premises?'

Joseph was silent.

'Father, these are indisputably Brossard's files and belongings. We are now searching for his car. If it's here, we'll find it. And if it's here, then it's very likely that you're hiding him somewhere on the premises. Now. Do you want us to pull this priory apart?'

'There is no one here.'

Sergeant Picot re-entered the cottage, accompanied by a corporal. 'No sign of it, sir. And nowhere they could hide it.'

Roux turned to Joseph. 'Father, I don't think it makes sense for you to continue to deny that Brossard has been here.'

'I did not deny it. I said, because our Prior is absent, I do not feel competent to discuss this matter with you. I will have to seek his advice. If you will allow me, I will try to reach him by telephone. As I told you he is presently in Rome.'

'No. I do not want you to use the telephone. We happen to know that Brossard is due to arrive in Villefranche today. We were told he was coming to this priory. Our information seems to have been correct. He came here but his car is not here at the moment. He may have gone out on some errand. We will wait for his return.'

'As you wish,' Joseph said. 'May we go now?'

'Just a moment,' Roux said. 'Sergeant, will you go with Father Francis? The gate opening is controlled from the telephone in his office.' He looked at

Joseph. 'The Sergeant will answer any calls from the gate.'

Joseph ignored this. 'Come, Father?'

Francis nodded. When both priests went out, Sergeant Picot following one pace behind them, Roux sat down again with the files. Somewhere, among these folders, could be the key to the years of flight and concealment. He opened the file marked 'Pardon' and began to read from a letter written by a Monsignor Gouet to Monsignor Le Moyne. 'It must be understood that the pardon is not, administratively, a personal decision on the part of the President. Doubtless, the President is well disposed in this matter, but he will do nothing without first obtaining the opinions of the Interior and the Justice Departments.'

As Roux read these lines, the corporal came running up the path, carrying a cellular telephone. 'For you, sir.'

'Roux here.'

'Robert, it's Daniel. Something fantastic has just come in on my computer. You haven't found him yet, have you?'

'No, but he's been here. We found his gear.'

'Robert, leave your men in place. But for God's sake, get down here yourself. Quick.'

CHAPTER TWENTY-SEVEN

'But who's going to re-imburse us for the loss of trade? It had nothing to do with us, this thing. We have customers coming this evening. We can't afford to be closed.'

Inspector Sarrat turned away from the proprietor

and looked at the two gendarmerie officers. 'What do you think, Colonel? As far as the police work is concerned, we can be cleared up by tonight. Is there anything special you need?'

Roux shook his head. 'No. That's fine. I'd like to go down to the morgue now and look at the body.'

'Of course. I'll phone and tell them you're coming.'

Roux turned back to Max Pellan. 'So you knew him well? A regular, when he was in Villefranche?'

'Yes, he was sort of a regular, but I just knew him as some old guy, retired, name of Pouliot, a cheapskate. He never talked about himself, not that I was interested.'

'The envelope?' Roux said. 'Do you remember anything special about it?'

'It was a registered letter,' Madame Pellan said. 'From Paris, I think. He was always here the day it came. He'd worry if the post was late.'

'And the man he killed?'

'Never seen him before,' Max said. 'He came in, ordered a beer, and went to the toilet while I was pouring it.'

Roux turned back to Inspector Sarrat. 'And that statement you found on the body, will it be possible to let us have a copy?'

The Inspector took a sheet of paper from the pocket of his anorak. 'I've already made copies for the reporters. Here you are.'

Later, as they drove up to the lower Corniche road, in the gendarmerie jeep, Daniel Dumesnil began to laugh. 'No conspiracy there,' he said. 'Full co-operation from the police. Maybe we've misjudged them.'

'It was the same thing in Salon,' Roux said. 'Inspector Cholet couldn't have been more helpful.

182

Whoever's shielding Brossard is in Paris, high up, maybe even the Prefect. And saying nothing to these local *flics*. That manifesto. Read it to me again, will you?'

Dumesnil took the sheet of paper from his briefcase:

STATEMENT

COMMITTEE FOR JUSTICE FOR THE JEWISH VICTIMS OF DOMBEY

This man is Pierre Brossard, former Chief of the Second Section of the Marseille region of the milice, condemned to death *in absentia* by French courts, in 1944 and again in 1946, and further charged with a crime against humanity in the murder of fourteen Jews at Dombey, Alpes-Maritimes, June 15, 1944. After forty-four years of delays, legal prevarications and the complicity of the Catholic Church in hiding Brossard from justice, the dead are now avenged. This case is closed.

'But it's not,' Roux said. 'Far from it.'

*   *   *

The body in the morgue was rolled out for their inspection. Roux bent to look at the face.

'Luckily, our office got him on the computer file before our friends the Paris police could wipe him off,' Dumesnil said.

'Good. Who is he?'

'Benrehail Ben Said, who goes by the name of Tomas Said, son of a Harkis sergeant who turned

183

robber in Marseille and was shot by the police in a hold-up in '74. The son followed in his footsteps and was arrested twice, working for Muhammad Remli, in Paris.'

'A drug *caïd*,' Roux said.

'That's right. This kid was believed to be one of Remli's hit men. Turned informer, but Remli doesn't know about it. Paris let him go after three months.'

'So he's a professional. Hired by this Jewish group. That's odd, isn't it? Why are they hiring professional killers and giving them Jewish names and documents? It doesn't add up.'

'I agree,' Dumesnil said. 'I rang the DST before you came down from the priory. They've never heard of this group. And they're pretty *au courant* in these matters. I got the same answer from the Wiesenthal Centre. Absolutely unknown.'

'Let's go back a little,' Roux said. 'You're Brossard, you've just killed another would-be assassin. You know by now, whoever this group is, they've followed you from Salon and they know you're staying at the priory in Villefranche. If you're as smart as Brossard you'll realize the assassin picked you up when you arrived at the priory this morning and followed you down to the old town. Brossard shot him around one-fifteen, according to the owner of the Bar Les Antilles. Brossard may then have driven back to the priory and seen your men in uniform, waiting at the turn of the road.'

'The stakeout wasn't in place until one-forty-five,' Dumesnil said. 'So, maybe he didn't see them. Maybe he didn't go back to the priory? Or do you think he'll try to sneak back in there later today? He might. And he won't see a stakeout this time.'

Roux shook his head. 'We've lost him, Daniel. I

184

know it. Let's keep the stakeout in place for another twenty-four hours. But I'm taking Brossard's files back to Paris tonight. I've got a lot of reading to do. And I'd better be quick.'

CHAPTER TWENTY-EIGHT

The building was on the Boulevard Jean Jaurès, just off the narrow winding streets of the old town of Nice. It had been put at the disposition of the Fraternity of St Donat by the Mayor of Nice, against the advice of the Bishop, who warned the Mayor that Dom Olivier Villedieu, the Prior General of the Fraternity, had chosen to follow Monsignor Lefebvre, the former Archbishop of Dakar who believed that, with the abandonment of the Latin mass and the changes that followed Vatican II, Rome was no longer the true Church. As a result, the Fraternity's house on the Boulevard Jean Jaurès was largely inhabited by priests improperly ordained in the eighties by Monsignor Lefebvre at his headquarters in Econe, Switzerland, in open defiance of the Vatican. And while few clerics or laymen had followed Dom Olivier and Monsignor Lefebvre in open rebellion, the Fraternity had certain sympathizers. Among these were the Chevaliers de Ste Marie, an order in which Dom Olivier held high rank.

So, now, and always, the Prior General was, for him, a brother in arms. More than that, Dom Olivier had, over the years, openly proclaimed to other clerics that: 'To shelter Pierre Brossard is not a question of sheltering someone under the Church's

185

laws of asylum. Pierre *must* be helped and protected because he is the victim of a plot by enemies of the true faith.' Thus, Dom Olivier and the priests of the Fraternity of St Donat were in a special category. There was no question of their heeding the Cardinal Primate's instructions. Here he would be welcomed as of old.

And the welcome was immediate. Embraced by Father Rozier, the *père hospitalier*, he was then led into the printing shop to be embraced again by Fathers Paul and Guy-Marie. And then, at last, up two flights of stairs to the cluttered study where Dom Olivier rose from his desk, peering at him through eyes weakened by cataracts, and then, recognizing him, came forward, arms extended to hug him in a brotherly embrace. 'Pierre! God bless you. How are you?'

'Well enough, thank you, Father. And you? You're looking well yourself.'

'God is good,' Dom Olivier said enigmatically. He was known to suffer from prostate cancer but it was not something he talked about. 'So, you're still playing at hide and seek?'

'Exactly so, Father Prior.'

'Do you know that we pray for you nightly, Pierre? You'll need our prayers now, more than ever.'

'Very true, Father.'

'Yes, I've been reading about this woman judge in Paris. And Delavigne! What a coward he is, what a disgrace! I must say his actions confirm everything Monsignor Lefebvre has said about the perfidy of Rome.'

'Alas, Father, his edict is having an effect. I'm being turned away at every door.'

'Pierre, this door will always be open to you. Good

to have you with us. And now, if you'll excuse me, I have work to do. I'll see you at supper.'

Father Rozier brought him up to a small room at the top of the house. 'Can we help you with your luggage?'

'I'm afraid I left it behind in Villefranche. It may be a few days before I can reclaim it.'

'How's that?'

'When I arrived at the priory of St Michel des Monts this morning, I left my luggage there and went down into the town. When I came back up there was a gendarmerie jeep parked near the entrance. So I turned round and came on here. Without my luggage, I'm afraid.'

'We can give you some night clothes, a razor, whatever you need for now.'

'Thank you. I'll ring Villefranche tomorrow and try to find out if my suspicions were correct. But in the meantime it's better to stay away.'

'Are you hungry? Would you like something to eat?'

'No, no. But may I use the telephone a little later? It's on a private matter.'

'There's a phone one floor down, in the bindery. I'll see you're not disturbed.'

'Thank you. Thank you very much.'

'Not at all. Just let me know when you need it.'

When Father Rozier left he was at last able to lie down on the narrow monk's pallet. He held his hands up, examining their tremor. Above him, framed in the narrow skylight, the pitiless blue Provençal sky. Sometimes it's as though I see an eye in that sky, watching me, judging me. But what did I do wrong? Everything I do is to defend myself. What's wrong with that?

He stared again at the rectangle of sky. Beyond that blue, beyond the invisible stars, beyond the sun, Who sees me, Who judges me, Who plans my fate? Was I right? Was that boy the same boy I saw in Aix? In the toilet, lying there in piss and blood with his cock hanging out; when I pulled his head up I only saw the face for a moment, before Max came running. I shot him in the back not knowing, because I couldn't take that chance, could I? And I was right to shoot. He had a gun.

The gendarmes, that's something else. If they're waiting for me and I don't turn up, sooner or later they'll go inside and talk to Joseph. Who knows what he'll say to them? They might search the place and find my suitcases, my files. I can't even phone to find out. The priory phone will be tapped. Vionnet's the one to call. He's *got* to get me out. I've got to tell him what happened today. He's supposed to protect me. Take a pill. I've got to calm down. Rest. Rest.

CHAPTER TWENTY-NINE

The Caves des Saussaies vineyard was located on the Route Nationale between Vaison la Romaine and Nyons, and consisted of a modest farmhouse, a garage, two bottling and storage barns and, at the entrance, a fading sign: *Dégustation des Vins*. The wine-tasting room was similarly modest, a small shed with a bar counter, a rack of glasses and some bottles of the vineyard wine, an inexpensive Côtes du Ventoux. Tourists were not encouraged to stop and sample it. However, from time to time when serious buyers were in the area, the owner, former

Commissaire Vionnet, would drive over from Avignon to host a special tasting, for which Marie-Ange Caillard, the wife of Paul Caillard, the vineyard's manager, was expected to provide hors-d'oeuvres.

The potential buyers this afternoon were from a supermarket with headquarters in Orange. They arrived shortly before 6 p.m. Commissaire Vionnet had been waiting for them since four-thirty and was in a testy mood. However, he put a good face on it, and set out to be charming. Marie-Ange brought in the hors-d'oeuvres, then she and Paul withdrew to the farmhouse kitchen.

'It could be a big order,' Paul told her. 'I hope it goes well in there.'

But after fifteen minutes, the phone rang in the kitchen and when Paul answered a man's voice, anxious, hurried, said, 'Commissaire Vionnet, is he still there?'

'Yes.'

'This is Paris. Can you get him for me?'

'He's busy at the moment,' Paul said. 'If you give me your number I'll ask him to call.'

'No. No number. Tell him it's Inspector Pochon.'

Paul put the phone down and went into the wine-tasting shed. The Commissaire and the potential buyers were looking at some figures.

'There's a call from Paris, sir. An Inspector Pochon.'

He saw the Commissaire hesitate, then turn to the buyers. 'I'm sorry about this. I won't be a moment. Paul will help you with any questions about the wine itself.'

Marie-Ange saw the Commissaire come into the kitchen. He picked up the phone then looked at her.

189

'It's all right, sir,' she said. 'I'm just leaving.'

She went into the sitting room which adjoined the kitchen. The television set was on, but the sound had been turned down. It was a football match. She had no interest in football but she sat on the sofa, pretending to look at the set. She could hear the Commissaire on the phone next door.

'When?'

He was silent for a moment, then: 'It was on television? And *Nice Matin*, how did they get hold of the letter?'

And then: 'Where did you find these idiots? A seventy-year-old man and he picks them off like crows!'

He was silent again, and then he said, 'The patron met this kid, don't you remember? We sent him over to the apartment the night before he left Paris. The patron was worried about this very thing.'

He listened for a long moment. Then:

'No, it's too late for that. I'd better go home at once. He may ring me tonight.'

She heard him hang up and then he called. 'Marie-Ange?'

She let him call twice. She didn't want him to know she'd been listening in.

'I have to get back to Avignon,' he said. 'I'll go in and speak to them now. But tell Paul not to worry. I think the deal's all set. They're going to give us a six-month trial in their stores in Orange. Paul can show them round if they want to look at the vines. And thanks for the hors-d'oeuvres. Very nice.'

Later that evening, when the buyers had gone, Marie-Ange said to Paul, 'I thought he was retired from the police?'

'Of course he is. He took retirement in '82.'

190

'That's funny. I heard him on the phone with that inspector from Paris. I didn't understand what it was about, but it sounded like a police case. There's some letter in *Nice Matin* that he's worried about.'

'No, no, he retired long ago,' Paul said. 'They're probably looking into some old case.'

'I don't think so,' Marie-Ange said. 'And he was really worried. I could tell.'

CHAPTER THIRTY

They said nine o'clock and Pochon knew better than to be late. He sat in his usual place in this anonymous café, filled with tourists. He looked out across the Place de l'Alma at the buses coming down Avenue Président Wilson. Usually the contact arrived by the 63 bus, but tonight was different. He had said, 'I'm in a red Peugeot 306 and I'll pull in at the bus stop. Stay in the café until you see me.'

And here it was, nine o'clock, a warm summer night, the tour Eiffel floodlit across the Seine, everything normal, as if it was any night. But it wasn't any night. Everything had gone wrong. And here on the stroke of nine was the red Peugeot pulling in just above the 63 bus stop. He got up, leaving his beer untouched, and went out like a condemned man, walking blindly into a red light as he hurried across the avenue. The contact had opened the car door and was watching him. When he got in, the little Peugeot took off fast, heading across the Seine.

The contact was the usual one, a man in his fifties, a lawyer, perhaps, cold and impersonal, with a dismissing voice. Now, he stared straight ahead,

191

silent, driving fast.

'You've read the papers, of course?' Pochon said. He knew it was a stupid thing to say, but he had to say something.

The contact nodded.

'The television got it wrong,' Pochon said. 'As per usual.'

The contact didn't speak. They drove past the Invalides and the National Assembly and turned into Boulevard St Germain. By then Pochon guessed where he was being taken. The patron's apartment was on the Rue St Thomas d'Aquin. Pochon had never been there, but he knew the address because Commissaire Vionnet told him the Harkis kid had been brought there to see the patron, just before they sent him to Aix.

He was right about their destination. Rue St Thomas d'Aquin, Number 6. Fourth Floor, Apartment Number 5. An old building, discreet, lifetime tenants, carpet on the stairs, mahogany apartment doors. No lift.

As they climbed the stairs he saw the contact look at his watch. When they reached the fourth-floor landing the contact said, 'We're three minutes early.' And hesitated. Then pressed the apartment bell. A uniformed servant opened, a man in his fifties wearing a formal yellow-and-black-striped waistcoat. He did not ask their names but nodded to them to follow. Pochon went along a corridor in which Roman busts sat in wall niches, past a big drawing room, with a grand piano, large oil paintings, heavy antique furniture, oriental carpets. On the opposite side of the corridor was a dining room, its long mahogany table set with one elaborate place setting, crystal glasses, decanter, flowers. The patron had not yet had his supper.

The servant now knocked discreetly on a door at the far end of the apartment before opening it to show them into a large library room furnished with leather armchairs and a sofa, its high walls lined with bound volumes and, in the centre of the room, a great teak desk littered with papers. In a corner, a small television set was turned to a news programme: the American CNN. The very old man sitting by the set clicked off his remote and stood up. He nodded to the contact, then waved them to the sofa and chairs at the far end of the room, under a large set of windows heavily curtained in red velvet.

'Gentlemen, thank you for coming.' His voice was soft and charming but Pochon felt a hidden chill behind the politeness of tone. He waited until the old man was seated before sitting down himself. Pochon was not one to be impressed but now he was eight feet away from a man he had last seen in '61 in the main courtyard of the *préfecture*, when he, Pochon, was a young lieutenant. This old man was Maurice de Grandville, Paris Prefect of Police under General de Gaulle, who had proved his loyalty to the General by putting down a massive Paris demonstration by Algerians protesting de Gaulle's policies in their country. It was a famously brutal police action, which, the press said, left two hundred Algerians dead. Pochon, who had been part of it, well believed this figure. He had himself, at the end of that day, seen his fellow *flics* toss dead bodies into the Seine.

But, of course, the ex-Prefect wouldn't worry about that. This old man had all his life moved in elite circles, from his early years as a high official, working for Maréchal Pétain in Vichy, to an equally high position in the Resistance, when that seemed the

193

better option. In the post-war years he had served as a minister in two successive French governments and had acted as the friend and confidant of presidents and premiers. De Gaulle, in gratitude for his ruthless loyalty, had kept him on as Prefect for six years after the Paris killings. Now eighty years old, with a record of past actions requiring judicial investigation, which, over the years, had accumulated thirty tomes of evidence, without his ever spending a night in prison, he had outlived the statute of limitations on his former deeds. Except for one, the one that had shadowed his long career. In the years of German Occupation, as Secretary General of the *préfecture* of the Gironde, he had facilitated his SS colleagues by organizing a series of French deportation trains which sent sixteen hundred people, including two hundred and forty children, to their deaths in Nazi extermination camps. For this action there was no statute of limitations. The crime against humanity.

Pochon looked at the old face, loose with the folds of age, at the hand stiff as a claw, a cigarette smouldering between the index and second finger, at the dark ministerial suit, the red dot in its lapel the *boutonnière* of a Commander of the Legion of Honour. Money had been paid over the years to Commissaire Vionnet, to Pochon, and to the man they had helped protect. Money had been paid to lawyers, perhaps to judges. Favours had been given and favours asked for, involving high civil servants and politicians of differing parties. All to protect this old half-corpse. And now, because of Pochon's error, this old man, at the end of his life, was at risk as never before.

The old man's hand went to his mouth and he drew deeply on his cigarette. 'We know the news,' he said.

'There's no point in discussing what has gone wrong. Incredible as it seems, you, Inspector, have sent two total incompetents to perform an action which would have seemed to me, on the face of it, to be relatively simple. The precautions we took to be sure that this action would never be traced back to us have now, I dare say, become the very facts that may destroy us. They will draw attention to my own case and this attention will certainly increase if the gendarmerie succeed in finding Brossard. A search warrant was issued recently without our knowing it, despite the fact that this would seem impossible in view of our connections in the *préfecture* and in the DST. This *juge d'instruction* trusts no one. Where is Brossard at present?'

'I am not quite sure, sir. We are almost certain that he is under the protection of an *"intégriste"* group of clerics in Nice.'

'You are not quite sure,' the old man said. 'What does that mean?'

'The Commissaire hopes to hear from him tomorrow morning at the latest. In the past, he has always informed the Commissaire at once, when he changes his address.'

'The past is no criterion for judging how he will act tomorrow,' the old man said. 'He must be frightened. Or perhaps that is not the right word. He is a cunning criminal, with a criminal's sense of danger, as he has proven clearly in the past two weeks. Now, I have two questions for you, Inspector. The first question is: Have you dealt directly with Brossard? Does he know you by sight?'

'Yes, sir. I worked with him in the days when you yourself were in the *préfecture*. Because of his past, he was trusted by right-wing groups in the days of the

195

OAS. We used him as a paid informer.'

'The Algerian years were a long time ago. Have you, personally, kept in touch with him since then?'

'Yes, sir. I talked to him, in person, some five years ago.'

'Then he knows you. Good. He would not see you as a possible assassin.'

And, at once, Pochon knew why he had been brought here.

CHAPTER THIRTY-ONE

'Aren't you coming to bed?' Rosa said.

'In a little while,' he told her. 'I'll be in, in a little while.'

It was after eleven. He knew there was no point in his waiting up for Brossard any longer. He'll never call this late at night. But where *is* he? Surely he knows that I've heard it on the news?

And then, at eleven-twenty, the phone did ring. He ran out into the hall to get it. It was Paris, again. He listened carefully.

'No, I haven't heard from him yet,' he said. 'He'll call, but I don't think it will be tonight. I'll ring the priory in Nice first thing in the morning. He's got to be there. Where can I reach you in the morning?'

'They have me booked on a flight that gets into Nice at ten. That's the earliest flight. All they said was, it's up to you and me to finish it. By tomorrow night, if possible. Shit! Why me?'

'You have no choice,' he said. 'They're right, of course. He knows you. He'll not run away from you. But first we'll have to think how to get him out of that priory.'

'If he's there.'

'He must be there,' the Commissaire said. 'Wait. I have an idea. The last time I spoke to him he asked if I could get him a passport. If I reach him tomorrow, I'll tell him you're going to arrange it for him. That way we can set up a meeting between the two of you. When do you land in Nice?'

'The flight's due in at ten.'

'Call me then.'

CHAPTER THIRTY-TWO

The lamp, lit for so many hours over Colonel Roux's writing table, now cast its yellow beam against a new cold light cutting into the room in long strips through the half-opened shutters. The worn leather trunk sat at his feet and, on his left, methodically stacked, were fifteen children's exercise books, and a dozen folders, filled with copies of letters, newspaper clippings, official forms, most of them yellowing and stiff with age. Several of the folders contained typewritten copies of letters written over a thirty-year period by the indefatigable Monsignor Le Moyne, letters of exquisite courtesy, filled with sycophantic phrases, devout injunctions and elaborate salutations, letters to the President of the Republic, to ministers of state, to the former Cardinal Primate of France, to the Secretary of State of the Vatican, to the Auxiliary Archbishop of Paris, to *juges d'instruction*, to prefects of police, to criminal lawyers, to former Resistance workers, to mothers superior of a dozen convents, to abbots of great monastic orders and to humble country priests.

Almost forty years of pleadings, of legal manoeuvrings, of delays and disappointments, from the early years when the subject of these letters was an unknown and unimportant wartime collaborator who, his supporters insisted, had suffered and atoned for his sins and now deserved to be forgiven for reasons of Christian charity and national reconciliation, a steadily persistent campaign which led to the triumph of a presidential pardon in 1971 and, one year later, because of the publicity given by *Le Monde* to that pardon, to a sudden interest in his case and the grave shock of a new charge of a crime against humanity, a charge that escalated and magnified the manoeuvres, the pleadings, the level of debate. The man who owned this trunk had not only kept copies of all letters and newspaper clippings relating to the affair, but had, in children's exercise books, listed names and addresses of important religious and civil figures, the location of convents and abbeys throughout France. In a separate book, Roux found the names of certain abbeys set out, twelve or more to a page, accompanied by tiny hieroglyphics which, towards morning, he began to study, hoping to break their code. He was weary and confused for his reading had begun that evening, the moment he boarded the plane from Nice to Paris, and continued after a hurried supper with Claire. Now, in the grey light of dawn, despite the urgency of his task, he felt he must admit defeat. In this labyrinth of paper, there was no biography, no clear record of Brossard's movements, no hint of why so many influential religious and lay figures had devoted so much time and effort to protect this criminal hiding from his fate.

And then, as he stared dully at the last entries in the exercise book that contained the lists of abbeys and priories, he noticed, among the tiny notations, the letters CSM and, beside them, a stroke accompanied by a single letter. The letters varied M/ J/ J/ A/. Suddenly, he turned back to the previous page and saw ten addresses of abbeys and convents, marked each with the letters CSM and then a single letter. CSM. Chevaliers de Ste Marie. The payments! And the single letters could denote the month of payment. Again he turned back. The abbeys on an earlier page were listed in slightly different order, initialled for different months. But, for the most part, the places were the same. He turned back again and found a similar list of abbeys on the page before that. Again the order had been changed and the months of visitation, if that was what these letters meant, changed from year to year. Suddenly excited, he turned to the latest entries. This page had not been completed. The letters CSM had not been filled in beside the names of the last two religious establishments. The penultimate entry was the Prieuré St Christophe. The monthly initial had been filled in. It was M. Today was May the 10th. The last entry was Prieuré de la Fraternité Sacerdotale de St Donat. There were no CSM initials, no monthly initial.

Roux looked at his watch. It was 6 a.m. He picked up the phone and dialled the operations room of the gendarmerie.

CHAPTER THIRTY-THREE

When Rosa Vionnet woke at 7 a.m., Henri was not in the bed. She knew at once that it had to do with last night's phone call. When she went downstairs to make breakfast, he was sitting out on the porch, staring into the car-park of the big Leclerc supermarket opposite. He did not look at her, or speak.

'Have you had your coffee?'

He did not answer. She went into the kitchen and turned on the gas. As she did, she heard him push his chair back and go into the parlour. He picked up the phone then replaced it on its cradle, without using it. He went back out on to the porch.

When she brought him his coffee and a *tartine* he spoke for the first time. 'Go up to the bedroom and wait till I call you. I have to use the phone.'

That probably meant he was going to call Paris. He never wanted her to hear his Paris calls. He told people that he was retired, but she knew he still worked for the *préfecture*. Sometimes he took calls from an Inspector Pochon. And talked to Pochon as if he was still Monsieur Le Commissaire and Pochon worked for him.

Anyway, she told herself, it's none of my business. But I don't like him getting upset. His blood pressure, those pills he takes, it's a worry for me. After all, he's seventy-five years old.

In the parlour, the Commissaire picked up the telephone and dialled the Nice number. Monks rose early.

'Prieuré St Donat, good morning.'

200

'Good morning, Father. I know this is early and I know it's unusual, but I am a friend of a guest who may be staying with you. A Monsieur Pouliot.'

'I am sorry. We do not have any guest staying with us at present.'

'But you know Monsieur Pouliot? Monsieur Pierre Pouliot. It's very important that I reach him. My name is Saussaies. Henri Saussaies. He told me he would be coming to visit you at this time. So, if he does turn up, would you tell him to telephone me at once. It's urgent. He has my number.'

'I'm sorry, sir, but we are not expecting anyone and I'm afraid we don't know anyone by that name.'

'Well, thank you anyway, Father. And if, by any chance, he does turn up?'

'I'm sorry, sir. I'm afraid you've been misinformed. Thank you. Good day.'

Of course they are not going to tell me he's there, or admit they know him. But Monsieur Saussaies. If they tell him that name, he'll know.

CHAPTER THIRTY-FOUR

The priests of the Fraternité St Donat ate all of their meals in silence. The refectory was a bare whitewashed room furnished with two rough tables and benches and a Romanesque crucifix that dominated the main wall. The kitchen monks brought in a large basket filled with thick chunks of *gros pain* bread baked that night in the priory ovens. The coffee was bitter as chicory and served in soup bowls. It was, he knew, a penance to stay more than a week or two in this retreat, for Dom Olivier, as part of his crusade against the venality and false doctrines of the modern Church, had established here an almost medieval routine of prayer and mortification, humble food and strict adherence to the old religious rules of fasting and abstinence.

He looked around him. No one spoke. He reached for and began to eat one of the hunks of bread, but his dentures could not manage to bite through the crust. He saw Dom Olivier enter the refectory and take a seat at the head of the table, bowing his head to say a long private grace. When the Prior had finished he raised his head, looked down to where his visitor sat and pointed his index finger in his direction, in a sign which might be interpreted as some sort of warning, but was, more likely, a silent salutation.

Newspapers, other than those religious tracts published in Econe, were not available in the priory, nor was there any television. He would have to go outside to learn what the press said about yesterday's shooting. He planned to do that before ringing the Commissaire. The coffee was not only bitter, it was tepid. He put down his bowl and ostentatiously made the sign of the cross, to show that he had finished, a tactful gesture in a religious house such as this one. But when he rose to leave the table, Dom Olivier again caught his eye and again raised his hand. He's signalling me that he wants to see me. He nodded obediently to Dom Olivier then went outside into the hallway and stood waiting before a painting of St Sébastien, transfixed by arrows.

A few minutes later Dom Olivier came out of the refectory, walking with the too-certain step of the half blind. He nodded, indicating that he was to be followed, and led the way along the hallway and into a small parlour used as a waiting room when visitors

202

came to speak to one of the resident priests. Then, surprisingly, from the deep lap pocket of his robe, Dom Olivier produced a newspaper.

'I did not want to alarm you, Pierre. Poor man, you have troubles enough. But have you seen this story?' He looked at the paper, *Nice Matin*, Front Page:

MYSTERIOUS MURDER IN VILLEFRANCHE

Armed Canadian shot dead in bar

Leaflet found on body—link to Brossard Affair

He moved quickly to the text of the leaflet, which was printed in full in the newspaper report. The same message as in Salon. So I didn't make a mistake. I killed the killer.

But as he read, he was aware that Dom Olivier was watching him. He looked up at the Prior. 'My God!' he said. 'Who *was* this man?'

'A Canadian passport was found on the body,' Dom Olivier said. He pulled a chair out from under the parlour table and sat down as though exhausted. A trickle of sweat ran down his cheek. 'Do you believe in the Devil, Pierre?'

What is he talking about?

'The Devil, Father Prior?'

Dom Olivier produced a large red cotton handkerchief and wiped his face. 'Pierre, one of the reasons we have lost the true path is because the Devil, more than at any other time in history, has managed to conceal his ways and works. The people have forgotten that the Evil One exists. And, alas, the Church, the Papal Church, has not seen fit to remind them of his existence. If, indeed, the Papal Church *believes* that the Devil still exists. I am not sure of

203

that, as I am not sure of anything in connection with present-day Rome. But the Devil is behind this attempt to kill you. Do you not see that?'

'The Devil, Father Prior?'

'Yes, the Devil, Pierre. We know, and we have always known, that the Jews do not have the interests of France at heart and that they are still willing to sow dissension and feelings of guilt and blame, more than forty years after the German Occupation. I see that lust for vengeance as inspired by the Devil. Don't you?'

He nodded uncertainly. What was the Prior getting at?

'Of course you do,' Dom Olivier said. 'These Jews, whoever they are, sent one of their number from Canada to kill you. When he killed you, he would leave that leaflet on your body. And when your body was found there would be more publicity than ever before about your disappearance, which would give the Jews a new chance to bring up those old stories of the 1943 round-up in the Vél d'Hiver sports drome, and the deportation trains from Drancy and other places. Once again the charge of a crime against humanity would be made against certain politicians, men of dignity, men who held high positions, who now, in their old age, still face the threat of trial and prosecution. And again, through such trials, our country could be held up to shame in the eyes of the world. A pity that this leaflet was found on the body of the would-be assassin. But you didn't know about the leaflet, I suppose?'

He stared at this man, half blind, frail, his head nodding in an involuntary dodder, his hand absent-mindedly wiping his chin with that red kerchief. 'The leaflet, Father?'

Dom Olivier straightened up in his chair as though in pain. 'My back,' he said. 'It's such a trial at times. Yes, the leaflet. When you shot him, you didn't know there was a leaflet on his body. Or did you? I've been wondering. The man in Salon was a Canadian. Did you find a similar leaflet on his body?'

'I don't understand, Father Prior.'

The Prior, for the first time, smiled at him. 'You know our friend Dom André Vergnes, the Prior of the Prieuré St Christophe in Aix? Of course you do, Pierre. We both know him. He is a member of the Chevaliers. He stands quite high in that organization. I am myself a member of the Chevaliers and Dom André and I have remained friends despite our doctrinal differences. Last week he rang me up and told me he thought you would be visiting us soon. He said he felt it his duty to warn me of his belief that you killed that man in Salon. As I now believe you shot that man yesterday. No, no, don't look so alarmed, Pierre. In my opinion your defending yourself against an assassin is a wholly commendable action. Especially as the assassin was doing the Devil's work, I can only say, as I've said before, that you are one of us and that I will do my utmost to protect you against our enemies. But I am afraid for you, Pierre. Who is it who knows where to find you? Have you any idea?'

'No, Father Prior.'

'Have you thought of going abroad? Of leaving France? I know that in the past you did not want our enemies to force you into exile from the country you love. But now ... I don't know. What do you think?'

'I think it is something I should consider.'

'Good. Think about it. If you decide to emigrate perhaps we can help you.'

'That's very kind of you, Father Prior. In the
205

meantime, I have important lay friends who may have access to a Vatican passport.'

'I wouldn't count on any assistance from Rome, if I were you,' Dom Olivier said. 'None of us can count on Rome nowadays. The days of Pope Pius, God rest his soul, are history. He knew that the Germans were not the true enemies of religion. The present Pope does not.'

'Father Prior, my lay friends may have other sources. They know about these things. But if they fail me I will certainly be grateful for any help you can give.'

Dom Olivier rose shakily from his chair and advanced to embrace him. He felt the sick wet skin touch his cheek. 'We are all in God's hands,' Dom Olivier said. 'And I am sure that God protected you yesterday, as He has in the past. Now, I must say my mass. Would you like to join us in the chapel?'

He bowed his head in humble acquiescence. The call to the Commissaire would have to wait.

CHAPTER THIRTY-FIVE

'It's a long shot,' Roux said. 'But at the moment it's all I have.'

Judge Livi looked up from her study of the child's exercise book which Roux had given her. 'It's brilliant,' she said. 'And you have the address?'

'Yes, we turned it up at once. It seems the Fraternité is closely linked with Monsignor Lefebvre's headquarters in Switzerland. The DST keeps an eye on that prelate and his doings. The house, in which the priory is located, was given to the

Fraternité St Donat by the Mayor of Nice, *against* the advice of the local bishop.'

'Why would the Mayor do that, I wonder?'

'Another mystery,' Roux said. 'But if Brossard's hiding out there now, the Prior, one Dom Olivier Villedieu, is a man who will do everything to keep us from finding him.'

'But you'll find him,' Judge Livi said. She moved to a typewriter. 'I have great faith in you, Colonel. If you'll give me that address, I'll make up the search warrant.'

'Here you are.'

She began to type, then stopped. 'You know, now is the perfect time to bring Brossard in. With this latest killing the case will be more than political.'

'What do you mean, Madame?'

'You know what the media are like. They're not interested in history. Murder is a much more selling item than old wartime tales. A double murder, two dead assassins, and the stink of Church involvement. If you can bring Brossard in, it will be an international story and that will make it much easier for me to see that the other gentlemen charged with a crime against humanity are no longer protected by my superiors in the Justice Ministry and the Elysée Palace. Their trials will follow inevitably on Brossard's.'

'*If* I can find Brossard in time,' Roux said.

'What do you mean?'

'It's a race I could lose,' Roux said. 'Someone else wants to find him and kill him. Someone who knows him and his movements better than we do.'

'I've been thinking,' Judge Livi said. 'Why has he been paid a large sum of money regularly by someone in Paris? Someone who doesn't seem to have anything to do with the Church and the Chevaliers. The Chevaliers' stipend is 3,000 francs a month. Modest. A charitable donation. But this other payment seems to be a large one. What does that suggest to you?'

'Someone who's paying him for services rendered?' Roux said. 'Or paying to keep him quiet.'

'Someone who desperately doesn't want to see him caught and brought to trial,' Judge Livi said. 'And who could that be, do you think?'

'Some important personage who faces a similar charge?'

'Exactly,' Judge Livi said.

CHAPTER THIRTY-SIX

He knelt in the rear of the Fraternité's chapel but did not pray. On the altar Dom Olivier was saying mass, the Latin mass as it had once been celebrated in every country on the globe. But all that was ended. Now, the saying of the Latin mass was an act of rebellion against the Papacy and the present. Watching Dom Olivier perform the familiar movements, hearing the remembered Latin phrases, he was transported back through the decades to those days before the war, to that gentle France Charles Trenet sang about, that France now gone for ever. Today, at the end of his life, what was there to keep him in a France run to benefit *beurs* and *noirs*, a France where a presidential pardon could be overturned by some new law brought in by international Jewry?

It was in the course of that mass, here in the safe haven of Dom Olivier's protection, that he made his final decision. Even if the Commissaire refused to help with a passport, even if they refused to keep sending his payments, he would leave France. As he knelt here, he could reach into the fat money belt he wore at all times and touch part of his life savings, the payments he had thriftily hoarded over the years. With that, and the deposits he had made in a bank in Bern, he had enough to live on for some time.

The mass was ending. He rose with the others, genuflected to the altar and went out into the corridor, looking for Father Rozier, the *père hospitalier* who had promised to let him use the telephone. But when he went into Father Rozier's office, Father Rozier was not there. A very young priest sat at Father Rozier's desk.

'Are you Monsieur Pouliot?' the young priest asked.

'Yes, I am.'

'I didn't know where to find you,' the young priest said. 'I looked in your room.'

'I was at mass. What is this about?'

'A gentleman telephoned earlier this morning and asked for you by name. Of course I said we had never heard of you. But he seemed to know you would be here. A Monsieur Saussaies. He wants you to call him. He said you have his number.'

'Thank you. By the way, Father Rozier told me yesterday that I could use the bindery telephone and that I wouldn't be disturbed there.'

'Of course,' the young priest said. 'The bindery's not in use any more.' He rose from his desk. 'I'll show you the way.'

In the bindery on the third floor, the shutters were closed against the sun, leaving the room in almost total darkness. The young priest opened a shutter,

209

showed him where the telephone was, then withdrew, closing him in.

Avignon. He dialled. The Commissaire picked up on the first ring.

'Monsieur Pierre here, sir.'

'Where is *here*?' the Commissaire asked irritably.

'Nice, sir. I'm at the Prieuré St Donat. You rang earlier, sir?'

'Yes, I did. Where the hell have you been? Why didn't you phone last night?'

'It was difficult, sir. You know what happened yesterday?'

'Of course, I do. The whole damn country does.'

'I know, sir. That's what I wanted to talk to you about.'

'No, you listen to me,' the Commissaire said. 'The other day you mentioned us getting you out of France. I think the time has come for us to do just that.'

He felt a sudden rush of relief, a strange weakness as though he could weep. 'Sir, that's just what I was thinking myself. As soon as possible, sir. Would it have to be South America, sir?'

'South America?'

'A long time ago, you spoke of Bolivia, sir. I assume we might be helped by the Vatican?'

'That's ancient history,' the Commissaire said. 'You'll get no help from Rome nowadays. No, we'll arrange the passport ourselves. You remember Inspector Pochon?'

'Pochon? Yes, sir. You sent him to see me once.'

'That's right. And I'm sending him again. In fact, he'll be arriving in Nice later today. I've asked him to call you and set up a meeting at a location he'll pick. The meeting should take place tonight. And I don't want you to mention it to anyone, not even to your friend Dom Olivier. Is that clear?'

'Yes, sir. Sir, could I ask, what country are you thinking of sending me to?'

'Where do you want to go?'

'I don't know. Some place that's not full of *beurs* and *noirs*.'

'Well, you can discuss that with Pochon. We'll have to work quickly. I want to get you out of the country within the week. In the meantime, except for your meeting tonight with Pochon, you're not to go outside the door of the place you're staying. The newspapers and television have plastered your mug up all over the place. That's why your meeting should be after dark. When you go out tonight, make sure you're not followed.'

'Yes, sir.'

'All right, then. Wait for a call from Pochon. And tell the priests there to put the call through to you as soon as it comes.'

'Yes, sir. Thank you, sir.'

'Good luck,' the Commissaire said. 'Don't worry. You're going to be all right.'

When he heard the Commissaire hang up, he remembered that he had not asked him about the payments. They'll keep on paying me, won't they? I'll ask Pochon about that.

CHAPTER THIRTY-SEVEN

Roux arrived in Nice at 3 p.m. and was met in the airport lounge by Daniel Dumesnil. Both officers were in uniform. They shook hands, smiling at each

211

other, then went outside where a uniformed driver and jeep were waiting.

'I've had four men over there since ten o'clock this morning,' Dumesnil said. 'I checked with them fifteen minutes ago. So far, no movement of any sort. We're covering both exits to the priory as well as the front entrance on Avenue Jean Jaurès. I have a plainclothes man out front so as not to advertise ourselves.'

'Good.'

The jeep left the airport and drove along the Nice promenade. 'He may not be in the priory at the moment,' Roux said. 'He could be in town. But if he's staying at the priory he'll probably come back in by suppertime. After all, he's seventy years old.'

'But he still shoots straight,' Dumesnil said, and laughed.

'So, let's fix a time,' Roux said. 'If your men don't see any movement before 7 p.m., we'll assume that he's in the house. What time do you think they have supper?'

'Monks rise early,' Dumesnil said. 'I'd say they'd eat by seven-thirty, at the latest.'

'All right. We'll go in at eight.'

'And until then, what?'

'Until then we sweat.'

CHAPTER THIRTY-EIGHT

The midday meal was a slice of the priory's home-baked *gros pain* and a cup of what the priest on his left called fish stew. Grace was said by Dom Olivier himself, but he noticed that no food was placed in

212

front of the Prior.

'Is the Father Prior on a special diet?' he asked the priest.

'Dom Olivier is fasting,' he was informed. 'All of this week he eats only the morning collation.'

He looked at the greasy cup of dishwater in front of him. With food like this, fasting was not a penance. Normally, he could go off to a café and have a late lunch. But not today. He spooned a small piece of fish out of the cup but decided not to taste it.

'Monsieur Pierre?' It was Father Rozier. 'If you will go upstairs I'll put your call through.'

'Is it?'

'Yes. The name you mentioned.'

*　　*　　*

The bindery was dark. The opened shutter had been closed by someone since his earlier visit. He entered and saw a red light blinking on the telephone.

'Hello?' he said. 'Monsieur Pierre here.'

'Monsieur Pierre?'

'Yes.'

'You remember me, don't you?'

'Yes, very well. How do you do, sir?'

'Tell me. Do you have much luggage?'

'No, sir. None at all. I had to leave my bags behind in Villefranche. I didn't think it wise to go back and reclaim them.'

'I see. Well, that simplifies things. Whoever's following you these days seems to be pretty good at tracking your movements. So, as a first step, we're going to take you at once to somewhere entirely new. Now, listen carefully. When you leave tonight, tell your clerical friends that you are leaving. But nothing more.'

'What about my car, sir?'

'Don't go near your car. Forget about your car. You won't need it.'

'You mean, just leave it behind?'

'Yes, I mean just leave it behind! Do you realize the situation you're in? You may be followed tonight. They may know where you are. It's up to me to help you give them the slip. On no account must you leave the priory before our meeting. At 9 p.m. go out and take a taxi to this address. Do you have a pencil?'

'Yes, sir.'

'Café Corona, Rue René Clair, Number 7. I will be waiting for you there with a car and I'll drive you to a safe house where we'll keep you until the arrangements are completed.'

'The arrangements, sir?'

'The arrangements to get you out of France as quickly as possible. I hope to have them complete by the day after tomorrow.'

'But, sir, may I ask where? I mean, what country?'

'We'll talk about that tonight. Just do as I say. Have you got that address?'

'Yes, sir.'

'It's near the Château. You know where that is?'

'Yes, I do.'

'Good. I'll expect to see you about nine-fifteen. Now, don't worry. We'll take care of you. You'll be all right.'

'Café Corona. Nine-fifteen. Thank you, sir.'

*   *   *

When he put down the receiver he stood for a moment in the darkened room, then went to the shutters and opened them. The sun beat down, a blinding, bronze fireball. There was no wind. Next door to the *prieuré* on a dusty roof terrace, a line of washing, women's slips and men's shirts, hung limp and ghostly in the noonday heat. Exile is like jail. I'm French, I'm pure French, I only speak French, it's my France, *my France*. I don't want to leave it.

A blonde girl came out on to the roof terrace, next door. She wore shorts but no top. He watched her as she bent over with a watering can, wetting down a long trough filled with flowers. He felt a slight erection as he studied her naked breasts. She straightened up, looked in his direction, then looked away. She didn't see me. But he closed the shutter.

In the end it's always the same ... The Jews win. Remember what Dom Olivier said. The Jews' lust for vengeance is the work of the Devil. He's wrong but he's right. The Devil isn't someone with a cloven hoof and a forked tail. The Devil is the Jews.

CHAPTER THIRTY-NINE

Two official vehicles were waiting outside headquarters. Roux had ordered them up under cover of a raid on a factory employing illegal immigrants. No one, not even the men in the vehicles, knew where they were headed. Nice was as dangerous as Paris. There must be no possible leak. If the police here got wind of this, he could lose his man.

At five minutes past eight, the two vehicles arrived at the front entrance to the Prieuré St Donat. The plainclothes man on watch there joined them. By walkie-talkie the two men guarding the rear entrances were alerted that the raid was about to begin. When Roux pulled on the old-fashioned bell pull, a loud electric buzzer sounded within the building. He rang again. He expected them to be slow. He expected them to spirit Brossard out of sight. But in a surprisingly short time the door was opened by a middle-aged priest.

'I'm Father Rozier, I'm the *père hospitalier* here. Who did you wish to see?'

'I would like to see the Prior. I have a search warrant for these premises.'

'The Prior? Dom Olivier is in the chapel at present. The rest of us are having our supper, but Dom Olivier is fasting as an act of special devotion. I'm sorry. You wouldn't be interested in that. I was just trying to explain why we shouldn't disturb him.'

'We don't have to disturb him,' Roux said. 'Here is the warrant. My men will start the search.'

Father Rozier put up his hands, refusing to take the warrant. 'If you will come with me, Colonel, I think we had better speak to Dom Olivier.'

Roux turned to Sergeant Picot and the two corporals. 'Wait here.'

As he followed Father Rozier down the corridor, they passed the refectory. Twelve priests sat at a long refectory table, with bowls of food in front of them. No one was eating. All stared at him as he followed Father Rozier into the small chapel. There, kneeling in the centre aisle, facing the tabernacle on the altar, Roux saw a tall, frail old man, his arms outstretched in the painful posture of cruciform devotion. Father Rozier went up the aisle, bent down and whispered in the old man's ear. The old man made the sign of the cross, then rose, genuflected and came down the aisle towards Roux.

'If you please?' he said, in a halting voice. 'I would prefer it if we went outside.'

His walk was uncertain, his hand trembled as he dipped it in the Holy Water font at the chapel exit. As a matter of politeness, Roux followed suit and made the sign of the cross before going out into the corridor. The Prior looked at the uniformed gendarmes waiting there.

'What is this about?' he asked.

'We are looking for a man named Pierre Brossard. We have reason to believe that he may be here.'

'Pierre Brossard,' the Prior said. 'I know him well. He has been a welcome guest here in the past. But, for his sake, I am glad that you are wasting your time. He is not in this house at present.'

'Nevertheless, we must make a search,' Roux said.

'Of course you must,' the Prior said. 'You have to do your duty, as do we all. Now, if you will excuse me. Father Rozier, please help these gentlemen.'

He nodded and went back into the chapel.

'All right,' Roux told the men. 'Start with the floor below.' He turned to Father Rozier. 'That's the basement, isn't it?'

'Yes. This way. I'll show you.'

The search began. But slowly Roux's tension and excitement drained away. Something was wrong. Either they had a hiding place within this house which they felt sure he would not find or his hunch, which had seemed brilliant at 6 a.m., was false. But, if there was a hiding place, he must find it. In the next twenty minutes he and his team made a thorough, a total, search in every room, cupboard, corridor and crawl space within the building. They found nothing.

CHAPTER FORTY

'Are you all right?' He was breathing so heavily that he couldn't speak. He nodded. Yes.

'Keep down.'

They were on the roof now. The young priest who had rushed him up here from the supper table went forward, crouching, peered over the parapet at the street below, then signalled him to come closer. Gasping, his back in agony from his crouching position, he advanced, crab-like, across the roof terrace. The priest was now dragging a long wooden plank across the roof as they moved towards the space between their building and the one next to it.

'Hurry!'

The priest beckoned again, then rose up and slid the long wooden plank over the gap between the buildings. It wavered in mid-air, then settled with a thump on the gutter of the opposing building. Gasping, his heart pounding, he joined the young priest under the shelter of the parapet.

'The janitor next door works as our janitor too,' the young priest told him. 'He's helped us before. There's a rear exit from his building. People think it's blocked up, but it's not. Are you sure you're all right?'

'Yes.'

'You'll have to cross on that plank. I've checked the street. The gendarmes are at both rear and front entrances. It's a risk, but I don't think they have someone in the alley. You'll have to hurry. They could come up here at any moment.'

'I know.'

He eased himself up and crawled on to the plank. He could not trust himself to stand up. He was afraid of heights, always had been, and now, dizzy, his heart thumping, short of breath, he peered down into the narrow alley below. There was no one there. As he began to crawl across the space between the buildings the plank swayed frighteningly. He paused, then went on. The plank swayed again and he shut his eyes, clinging to its edges, trembling. Please God, help me! Help me!

'Go on. That's good.'

The voice of the young priest, behind him, whispering. He crawled forward. He opened his eyes and saw that he had almost reached the other side.

'Go on. Go on!'

He crawled forward once more and felt the stone of the other building's parapet burn hot on the tips of his fingers. He pulled himself over the parapet and slid down on to the roof. At once he heard a slithering noise as the young priest began to haul the plank back to the priory's roof. He got to his feet. The young priest paused in his hauling to wave to him and to point to a door on the roof terrace.

'Hurry!'

Stumbling, half running, he approached the door. As he did it opened and a man looked out, a stout young man in jeans and a stained white T-shirt, his face wreathed in a huge moustache. The man beckoned urgently, bringing him inside. The room he entered was the living room of an apartment erected like a ramshackle shed on top of the building's flat roof. Beyond this room he could see a bedroom, a small cooking area and, half hidden behind a beaded curtain, a toilet and bidet. The walls of the living room were plastered with old Riviera holiday posters and crude reproductions of paintings of Provençal scenes. The furniture was green rattan, sagging with age, and on the *chaise-longue* by the window a young woman lay, smoking a cigarette and staring at him with a curious mixture of contempt and indifference. She wore red shorts and a red halter. She was the girl whose bare breasts he had studied earlier that day. The moustachioed young man pointed to a chair.

'Take a seat, Monsieur. Are you all right?'

He sat, gasping, nodding his head, yes, he was all right.

'The Fathers have a bell signal, when they want to get in touch with me. That's how I knew you were coming,' the man said. 'I do the furnace work in their building. You're not the first they've sent over.'

'It's none of his business who they sent,' the young woman said. 'Anyway, can't you see he's ill? Get him a glass of water. Want a glass of water, grandpa?'

He nodded, yes. The young man went into the makeshift kitchen. The young woman eased herself off the *chaise-longue*, her shorts sliding up over her buttocks. She lit a new cigarette off the stub of her old one, then went outside.

'Here you are, Monsieur.'

He took the glass. 'Thanks. They said you have a way out of here?'

'I do. But what's your hurry? Wait till the *flics* have gone.'

He drank the water which tasted brackish. He did not have his pills. A searing pain cut like a sword into his chest, making him gasp. 'What is this building?' he asked. 'Are there other tenants?'

'No. It's all offices. We're the only ones who live here.'

The young woman came back in again. 'Two *flics*

220

just came up on the roof next door,' she said. 'I blew them a kiss. Gendarmes. They waved at me.'

'Are they still there, Mademoiselle?'

'No, no, they went back down. Don't worry, grandpa. They'll be gone soon.'

He leaned forward in the chair, putting the glass down at his feet. Pain came in waves. Fear came with it. My heart, is it my heart? No, no, I've had this before. It's nerves. Calm down.

The young man went over to the table near the cooking area and poured himself half a tumbler of red wine. 'What are you going to do? Will you go back to the Fathers' place?'

'It's none of your business what he's going to do,' the girl said.

'I was just asking. You know. Conversation?'

'No, I'm not going back,' he said. 'I'm going somewhere else. Can I get a taxi near here?'

'When you come out from downstairs, you'll be in an alley,' the young man said. 'Go to the end of the alley and you're in Rue Recamier. There's a taxi rank halfway down on the left.'

'Thanks. Do you have an aspirin, by any chance?'

'Cécile, do we have aspirin?'

'Over the sink.'

The young man brought him the bottle. He took two, swallowing them down with a drink of the brackish water. He looked at his watch. Eight-thirty-seven. 'Are you sure it will be safe?' he said. 'I mean, I can't wait too long. I have to be somewhere at nine.'

'It's safe,' the young man said. 'Nobody knows you can get out that way. Nobody but us.'

'Wait,' the girl said. 'I think I heard something.'

'What? What?' All of a sudden he was in a panic.

'Hold your piss, grandpa,' she said. She went

outside. He watched her walk to the edge of the parapet and look down. She came back inside. 'A colonel, no less,' she said. 'You must be important. Anyway, they're leaving.'

He stood up. 'So must I.'

The young man gulped down the rest of his wine. 'All right, here we go.'

He followed the young man out of the door. As he was leaving he looked back at the girl. She smiled at him. 'I've seen you before, you know,' she said. 'How did you like my tits?'

He pretended not to hear. The pain began to ebb as he followed the young man across the rooftop through a door and down a short staircase to the top floor of the building. It was dark here. The young man switched on a light and led him down a corridor to a service lift, pulling back the iron grille of the door and motioning him to get in. The lift went down four landings and stopped with a thump in the basement of the building. The young man then led him through a furnace room and into a second room filled with old propane gas tanks and empty wine bottles. He pulled aside a sheet of corrugated iron. Beyond, in the dying Provençal sunlight, he saw a narrow filthy alley, lined with dustbins. The young man turned to him, his lips opening in a wet smile under his huge curling moustache. 'There you are, Monsieur. The road to freedom. *Salut!*'

He shook hands with the young man. I should give him something. But his money was in the money belt and it was risky to show that to a stranger. Instead, he said, 'God bless you, my son. Thank you.'

He heard the corrugated iron sheet screech on the concrete as the young man dragged it shut behind him. The pain was almost gone. The alley stank of rubbish but he stood, eagerly breathing in the fetid air of freedom. It had been close, closer than at any time since the end of the Occupation. The pain had gone. He looked at his watch. Eight-forty-nine. Just enough time to find a taxi, drive to the Café Corona and put himself in Pochon's care. And now, at last, he accepted his fate. It was time to leave, time to stop running, time to sit in the sunshine of some foreign city, a glass in his hand, a servant to make his meals, no need to move, no need to look up and down each time he walked out into the street. I have won.

There was no one in the alley. Above in the narrow space of sky between the walls, the sun had darkened from bright orange to a deep blood red. In a moment it would be night in the streets of Nice. He walked on, short of breath, but confident. At the end of the alley, a street sign: *Rue Recamier*. And there, halfway down, as the young man had told him, the taxi rank.

The Café Corona was small, decorated in *Belle-Époque* style with electric lamps fashioned to look like gas brackets. They flickered and cast shadows so that at first he did not see Inspector Pochon who was sitting at a table in the rear and who waved to him across the room. Pochon did not get up from his seat, but offered his hand very much in the way *flics* did when they were dealing with you and knew you were in their pay.

'Any trouble? Get here all right?'

He sat down and told what had happened. Pochon, small, grey-haired, in his sixties, listened in distracted impatience, as though he had heard it all before.

'Typical gendarmerie procedure,' Pochon said. 'They never cover their arse. If I'd been raiding that priory, you wouldn't be sitting here now.'

223

'Well, I am here,' he said. 'What's the next move?'

'I'm going to drive you across the border,' Pochon said. 'I was going to do it tomorrow, but after what you've told me we'd better go tonight. We'll cross into Italy at Menton and sleep in Ventimiglia. No problem. I have police documents. The border guards will wave us through. By the weekend I should have your passport and visas.'

'Passport? What sort of passport?'

'French, of course. Look at you, you couldn't be anything but French.'

He laughed at that. 'But where are you sending me, Inspector?'

'What about Canada? That suit you?'

'Canada?' He felt a rush of relief. 'They speak French there.'

'Some of them, yes. All right. Let's get out of here.'

Pochon put money on the table and stood up. He was small, all right. About five feet two. A little Napoléon. 'Ready?' He barked it out like an order.

He nodded. As they went out into the street he thought: Canada. 'Inspector, there's something I wanted to ask you. My payments. You'll send them on, will you? It will be expensive, living there.'

Pochon looked at him and shook his head in irritation. 'Never mind that, now. The car is in the car-park behind this alley.'

He saw Pochon look up and down the street, then beckon him to follow. He saw the little man, shoulders hunched, striding into the murk of the unlit alley. And suddenly, the hackle of danger rose within him. He hesitated.

'Hurry,' Pochon said and turned to see what was keeping him.

Uneasy, he went into the dark. And in that

moment saw Pochon raise both hands, saw the gun, a moment before the first bullet hit him in the chest. The second bullet hit while he was on his knees.

In death, he saw the dead men, lined up in a row, their feet touching the cemetery wall. There were fourteen of them, one short of the number he had promised the Gestapo. Their Jewish name tags, tied around their necks, fluttered gently in the night breeze. He would have to step over them to reach the other end of the alleyway. But, on his orders, the execution squad had placed them close together, with not enough room to pass between them.

He fell forward, striking his head on the concrete walk. Pain consumed him but through it he struggled to say, at last, that prayer the Church had taught him, that true act of contrition for his crimes. But he could feel no contrition. He had never felt contrite for the acts of his life. And now, when he asked God's pardon, God chose to show him fourteen dead Jews.

Pochon took a flashlight from his pocket and shined it on the dead face. He then put on a pair of surgical gloves. There must be no fingerprints on the statement. He crouched down and, carefully, using two large safety pins, pinned the statement to the dead man's chest.